Puppies
in Peril

Pup at the Palace
Illustrations by Ann Baum

Dog at the Door
Illustrations by Jenny Gregory

LUCY DANIELS

Hodder
Children's
Books

A division of Hachette Children's Books

This bind-up edition published in 2011 by Hodder Children's Books

**Thanks also to C. J. Hall, B.Vet.Med., M.R.C.V.S., for reviewing
the veterinary information contained in this book.**

Pup at the Palace
To David Teale – a good friend to Animal Ark
Special thanks to Jennie Walters
Text copyright © 1999 Working Partners Limited
Illustrations copyright © 2000 Ann Baum
First published as a single volume in Great Britain in 2000 by Hodder Children's Books

Dog at the Door
Special thanks to Pat Posner
Text copyright © 1997 Working Partners Limited
Illustrations copyright © 1997 Jenny Gregory
First published as a single volume in Great Britain in 1997 by Hodder Children's Books

Animal Ark is a trademark of Working Partners Limited
Created by Working Partners Limited, London WC1X 9HH
Original series created by Ben M. Baglio

A Catalogue record for this book is available from the British Library

ISBN 978 1 444 90729 2

Typeset in Baskerville by Avon DataSet Ltd,
Bidford-on-Avon, Warwickshire

Printed and bound in Great Britain by
CPI Bookmarque Ltd, Croydon, Surrey

The paper and board used in this paperback by Hodder Children's
Books are natural recyclable products made from wood grown in
sustainable forests. The manufacturing processes conform to the
environmental regulations of the country of origin.

Hodder Children's Books
a division of Hachette Children's Books
338 Euston Road, London NW1 3BH
An Hachette UK company
www.hachette.co.uk

Pup
at the
Palace

One

'Can you see anything yet, James?' Mandy Hope called eagerly across the carpark of the Fox and Goose. Pushing back her blonde hair, she shaded her eyes against the early-morning sun as she gazed over towards her friend.

'Not a sign,' James replied, turning round from his look-out post by the side of the road. 'Do you think they've forgotten about us?' he asked anxiously.

'Now don't you go alarming everyone, James Hunter!' Mandy's grandmother, Dorothy Hope, said good-naturedly. 'I phoned up to check only yesterday, and there's a coach definitely booked for eight o'clock. We've got a little while to go until then.'

'The driver won't dare to be a second late, if he knows what's good for him,' said her husband, Tom Hope, smiling at Mandy. 'You know what your grandmother's like when she's in an organising mood. Terrifying!'

As a keen member of the Welford Women's Institute, Dorothy Hope had volunteered to arrange their summer sightseeing expedition to London. It would be a wonderful way to celebrate the new century, and everyone was looking forward to seeing the Millennium Dome.

When Mandy had heard about the trip, she'd immediately thought it would be the perfect holiday for her hard-working parents – not to mention herself! Emily and Adam Hope had been rushed off their feet earlier in the summer at Animal Ark, their veterinary practice in the small Yorkshire village of Welford. Things had quietened down a little now though, so they were taking a few days off and leaving Simon, the practice nurse, in charge. They'd offered to take James to London along with them, as his parents couldn't manage to get away just then.

'Is everyone here now, Gran?' Mandy asked, looking round the group that was waiting in the carpark. She recognised lots of faces, though the people she knew best were the pet owners who came to her parents' surgery.

There was Mrs Platt, whom Mandy had helped to adopt an abandoned poodle from the animal sanctuary. She had a son in London she wanted to visit, so she'd settled the little dog, Antonia, into kennels and come along. Next to her stood Miss Davy, who lived in the Old School House and kept a flock of hens in her large garden. She looked as immaculate as ever, from the top of her silvery-grey head to the tip of her shiny brown leather shoes. Beside her, Mrs McFarlane from the post office was talking nineteen to the dozen. Her husband was staying at home, so he would be looking after their budgie, Billy, and keeping the post office and shop running smoothly.

'Let me just find my list,' said Mandy's gran, looking through a sheaf of papers in her shoulder bag. 'I think there are a few more people to come.'

'You and that list!' teased her husband affectionately. 'I should think you know it off by heart, you've looked at it so many times.'

'Well, you only have to put up with me and my list for a little while longer,' Dorothy Hope replied smartly, pulling out a dog-eared sheet of paper. 'Then you'll have total solitude for a few days.'

'Now come on, love,' Mandy's grandad replied gruffly. 'You know Smoky and I will be counting the days till you get back.'

'Are you sure you won't be too lonely without us?' Mandy asked him, suddenly picturing her grandfather and the cat all on their own in Lilac Cottage. She put her arm through his. 'If you want to come along, I'm sure it's not too late.'

Her grandfather shook his head. 'I'd better not, love,' he replied. 'The tomato plants in my greenhouse are at a very delicate stage and they'll die for certain if I leave them now. Don't you worry about me – your gran's filled the freezer with food and I'll be out in the garden from morning till night. I shall be expecting a postcard, mind.'

'I'll send you one of Buckingham Palace!' Mandy promised, before rushing over to join James. She felt too excited to stand in one place for long.

James was still looking hopefully up the road.

'Surely the coach should be coming soon!' Mandy said to him. 'I can't wait to get going, can you?'

'No,' James agreed, taking off his glasses and giving them a polish. 'Though I hope Mum and Dad remember to give Blackie lots of walks.' He'd just said goodbye to his parents and given his excitable Labrador a big farewell hug. James spent a lot of time exercising Blackie and trying to train him, and Mandy knew he would miss his dog while they were away.

'We're going to have a great time,' she said encouragingly, trying to take his mind off things. 'Just think of everything we'll be seeing – Buckingham Palace, Madame Tussaud's, Piccadilly Circus, the Tower of London—'

'And the Millennium Dome,' James reminded her as he put his glasses back on, beginning to look a bit happier. 'I really want to look at the computer displays in the Mind Zone.'

'And you should get some great photos,' Mandy said, spotting a camera at the top of James's bulging rucksack. She knew how interested he was in photography.

'I didn't want to risk bringing my best camera along, so I've only got the Polaroid,' James told her. 'Still, at least we can see the pictures straightaway. I took one of Blackie just now so I'd have something to remind me of him while we were away.' He pulled a photo out of his inside jacket pocket and showed it to Mandy.

'Oh, doesn't he look sweet!' Mandy said, smiling at Blackie's appealing face as he looked out of the picture with his head on one side. 'Come on, let's go and show Mum and Dad. We might as well sit with them till the coach comes.'

She picked up James's rucksack for him and led the way over to where her parents were sitting on one of the benches outside the pub, chatting quietly together. Her mother's long red hair glinted like a sheet of copper in the sun.

As they approached, her father broke off in an enormous yawn, raising one hand up to his beard. 'Don't worry, Dad,' Mandy said, patting his knee as she sat down next to him. 'You can have a good long sleep on the coach.' She knew her father had been up most of the night, helping a cow that had had some difficulty giving birth.

'I can't wait,' Adam Hope replied, putting his

hand over Mandy's. He looked paler than usual, and there were dark circles under his eyes. 'I could do with a holiday now, that's for sure.'

'Look at this lovely photo of Blackie that James has just taken,' Mandy said, showing her parents the picture. 'Doesn't he look cute?'

'He's got that wonderful Labrador grin on his face,' her mother said. 'They really do seem to smile sometimes, don't they?' She laughed and gave the photo back to James.

Mr and Mrs Hope loved animals just as much as Mandy did, and she often thought they must have the best job in the world. She'd learned a lot from helping them in the surgery and, one day, she hoped to be as good a vet herself. The Hopes had adopted Mandy when she was a baby, and she couldn't imagine a better home than the one she'd found with them at Animal Ark.

They had only been sitting down for a few minutes before Mandy spotted what they'd all been waiting for. A white minibus was driving slowly down the Walton road. 'At last!' she cried as it swung into the carpark. 'Now we can get moving!' She jumped to her feet and gave her father a hand up from the bench. Then she and

James grabbed their rucksacks, her father took the suitcase, and the four of them went over to join the others.

The driver opened the door and swung himself down, pushing a pair of sunglasses up on top of his head. 'Glad you're all ready and waiting,' he said, as he unlocked the luggage compartment so the cases could be loaded in. 'Traffic's building up already. I'll just pack the bags and then we'll be off. Bill's the name, by the way.' He was a small, energetic-looking man, who obviously didn't believe in wasting time chatting.

'But there are two people who haven't arrived yet,' Dorothy Hope told him, hurriedly consulting her list. 'We can't go without them.'

Bill looked at his watch. 'Well, I can't wait for ever,' he said. 'I promised to get you to London by two o'clock, so two o'clock sharp it'll be. I pride myself on my punctuality.'

'Who else is coming?' Mandy asked her grandmother.

Before she could reply, James supplied Mandy with the answer. 'Walter and Ernie!' he exclaimed in surprise.

Two elderly men were walking over from the

short row of stone cottages behind the pub, each carrying a battered, ancient-looking suitcase.

'Ah, here they are,' Dorothy Hope said with relief. 'They must have been waiting at home till they saw the coach arrive.'

'I wouldn't have thought they'd want to go to London,' Mandy whispered to James. Walter Pickard and Ernie Bell lived a few doors apart from each other and they both usually stayed close to home, apart from the occasional shopping trip into the nearby town of Walton.

'Morning, one and all,' Walter said pleasantly as they approached, touching his flat cap in greeting. He was a large, gentle man – a retired butcher who had lived on his own since his wife died. Ernie Bell just nodded briefly, eyeing the coach and its driver suspiciously. He was more difficult to get on with than Walter, though Mandy knew that his grumpy manner hid a kind heart.

'We didn't know you were interested in the big city, Mr Pickard,' James said to Walter, but it was Ernie who replied.

'Think we're past it, do you?' he growled, reluctantly letting Bill take his suitcase and wedge it on top of Miss Davy's neat zip-up bag. 'You're as bad as that Ponsonby woman. Don't you start going on about too much excitement being dangerous at our time of life. She's not the only one who can go gadding off down south, you know!'

Mandy tried hard not to smile. She couldn't think of anything more certain to send Ernie off to London than Mrs Ponsonby telling him he shouldn't go. Mrs Ponsonby was always bossing everyone about and giving them advice they didn't want to hear. She wasn't so good at taking advice herself, though. Mandy often told her that Pandora, her fat Pekinese, needed less food and more exercise, but it was no good. Mrs Ponsonby still gave Pandora titbits and carried her everywhere. Things had only improved a little since she'd taken in a mongrel puppy, Toby, who encouraged Pandora to run around and play like a normal dog.

Lately, Mrs Ponsonby had been more annoying than ever. She'd been invited to a garden party at Buckingham Palace because of all her work for charity. Everyone in the village had heard about it at least twenty times. Somehow, over the last few weeks, Mrs Ponsonby had managed to get the words, 'When I'm in London . . .' and 'When I meet the Queen . . .' into every conversation she had had. The garden party coincided with the WI trip but, much to everyone's relief, Mrs Ponsonby had decided to drive herself down, rather than travelling by coach with the rest of them.

'We knew there were a few spare places on the trip,' Walter explained quietly to Mandy and James, 'but we didn't really think it was our sort of thing. And then Mrs Ponsonby told Ernie that she quite understood why he didn't want to go. London was no place for an old fellow like him, set in his ways. So we decided to come after all.' He gave them a wink.

'That's great!' said Mandy, starting to climb into the minibus. 'I'm glad you did.' Then a thought suddenly occurred to her and she whirled round, nearly sending James flying. 'But who's going to look after Missie and Scraps and Tom?' Walter had three cats, and then there was Ernie's cat, Tiddles, to consider too, not to mention his pet squirrel Sammy.

'Don't you worry,' Walter reassured her. 'We wouldn't go off and abandon them. That young lad from the pub is calling in twice a day to feed them, and he's in charge of Tiddles and Sammy, too. He came round yesterday and we showed him where everything was.'

'Of course! John's back now, isn't he?' Mandy remembered.

John Hardy was the son of Julian Hardy, the landlord of the Fox and Goose, and he came back to Welford from boarding-school every holiday. Living so close by, he was the ideal person to look after Walter and Ernie's pets.

'John's certainly going to be busy,' Miss Davy said briskly. 'He's feeding my hens as well, and shutting them up for the night. I hope he's going to take his duties seriously.'

Bang on cue, an upstairs window in the pub flew open, and John Hardy's tousled head emerged. As he waved to them, Mandy felt a twinge of jealousy. She'd have loved being in charge of all those animals! A fresh surge of excitement soon stopped her feeling too envious, though.

When everyone was finally on board, Bill checked his watch again and they set off. The minibus pulled slowly out of the carpark and started down the road on its long journey to London.

They had only driven a short distance when Bill suddenly gave a shout of alarm and slammed on the brakes so sharply that all the passengers were thrown forward. The book Miss Davy had just opened flew across the aisle, James lost his headphones and Mrs McFarlane nearly choked on her peppermint.

James leaned round the seats in front to look through the windscreen, then nudged Mandy without speaking. He pointed up ahead, and she followed his glance. In the middle of the road stood none other than Mrs Ponsonby herself, puffing and panting and red in the face. She had a large suitcase and a hatbox at her feet. Her Peke, Pandora, was tucked under one arm, and she was waving the minibus down with the other.

'Stop this bus!' she shouted loudly.

Two

'Really, driver!' Mrs Ponsonby said severely after Bill had opened the minibus door. 'What kind of speed is that for a narrow country lane? You nearly ran me down! Now, please take my luggage, but do be careful. The hat in this box is an original design.'

Bill gave her a long look, as though deciding whether to reply, and then shook his head. Glancing at his watch, he grumbled, 'No time to open the boot. You'll have to keep your case with you.' He yanked up the suitcase and stowed it between the seats. Mrs Ponsonby clicked her tongue in annoyance, then picked up her hatbox, clutched Pandora more firmly, and prepared to climb on board.

'Gran! You didn't tell us Mrs Ponsonby was coming,' Mandy hissed through to the seats in front, where her grandmother was sitting on her own.

'I didn't know she was!' came Dorothy Hope's horrified reply.

'Here – you can't bring that animal on to my minibus!' Bill told Mrs Ponsonby, having just noticed Pandora. 'What if it messes on the floor?'

'Pandora is not just an "animal", she is a pedigree Pekinese,' Mrs Ponsonby announced grandly. 'And she does not "mess" on the floor, I can assure you.' She pushed past him indignantly and sank into the empty seat next to Dorothy Hope.

Bill shook his head again. 'You'd better be right,' he muttered doubtfully, starting the engine and preparing to drive off.

'Poor Gran!' Mandy whispered to James, pulling a sympathetic face. She knew Mrs Ponsonby really got on her grandmother's nerves. Now she would have to sit beside her all the way to London, with no chance of escape.

'I thought Mrs Ponsonby was driving down later,' James whispered back. 'What's she doing here now?'

Together, they listened as Mrs Ponsonby explained to Dorothy Hope. 'I'd decided to take the doggies out for a little drive last night, but – would you believe it – the car just wouldn't start! And who knows if I could have got it fixed in time to drive to London on Monday. One simply can't take any risks when one is meeting the Queen!' She laughed and patted her hat, while Mrs Hope murmured something Mandy couldn't hear.

'Anyway,' Mrs Ponsonby went on, 'I remembered there were some spare places on your little expedition. By that time, it was too late to phone you and check, and I must have just missed you when I rang this morning. So Pandora and I set off to meet you on the road! How lucky there's an empty seat next to you, Dorothy. We can chat all the way.'

'Very lucky,' Mandy's gran echoed faintly.

'But where's Toby, Mrs Ponsonby?' Mandy asked, undoing her safety belt for a few seconds and leaning over the top of the seats to give Pandora a quick pat.

'Oh, I've left him with my sister,' she replied, turning round to smile graciously at Mandy. 'Toby is a delightful creature, of course, but he might be a little – shall we say – unpredictable, staying in a hotel. Not to mention at Buckingham Palace! I'm afraid the excitement would be too much for him. He might forget himself.'

Mandy caught James's eye and they both collapsed into giggles behind the seat backs at the thought of Toby forgetting himself during a garden party at Buckingham Palace.

'What about your hotel?' Mandy's gran asked Mrs Ponsonby, as though an alarming thought had just occurred to her. 'Can they fit you in over the weekend? I'm afraid our bed and breakfast is fully booked – Walter and Ernie are having to stay in a pub round the corner.'

'Don't worry about that, my dear,' came the reply. 'I phoned the hotel last night and they can squeeze us in for a few extra nights. After all, I don't really think a bed and breakfast is quite our sort of place, is it, Pandora? And as for a pub . . .' She shuddered.

'Well, I think it's great here,' Mandy said,

bouncing on the bed in the twin room she was sharing with her grandmother. 'Good choice, Gran!'

The Welford party were staying in small hotels, pubs or guest houses in Greenwich, not far from the Millennium Dome. Dorothy Hope had booked her family and friends into a large Victorian house called The Crow's-Nest in one of the narrow streets near the river. Mandy had held her breath as Bill steered the minibus expertly through the traffic. There were so many cars, and so many people! It was all very different from the quiet green fields and country lanes of Welford.

'There you are,' Bill said, as he parked opposite the guest house and checked his watch again. 'Five to two. By the time I've unloaded all your luggage, it'll be two o'clock precisely!'

Inside The Crow's-Nest, everything was ordered and calm. The place was run by a fair-haired Scotsman with a bristly ginger beard, who introduced himself as 'Alexander McPherson, though everyone calls me Mac'. He showed them all to their rooms before starting to take their luggage upstairs. Mandy's parents had a double room with a four-poster bed, which they were delighted with. Eileen Davy and Mrs McFarlane were sharing a twin room, while James was on his own next door to Mandy and her grandmother. Mrs Platt was staying with her son over in Wimbledon, though she was going to meet up with the others for their trip to the Millennium Dome.

'If you don't mind, love,' Dorothy said, sitting on the other bed, 'I think I'll have a bit of a rest now. Six hours of Mrs Ponsonby has nearly finished me off. Why don't you and James go exploring?'

'OK, Gran,' Mandy said. 'I can understand just how you feel!'

She shut the door quietly behind her and set off down the corridor to find James. Just like the bedrooms, its walls were hung with old maps and prints of sailing ships.

James's room was full of model boats, too. 'I bet Mac's been a sailor at one time or another,' Mandy commented, picking up an ornament on the chest of drawers. It was a bottle, with a tiny ship sailing along inside it. 'How on earth did that get in there?' she wondered, fascinated.

James shrugged. 'Well, he certainly loves the

sea,' he said, laying his books out on the bedside table. 'Did you see the ship's wheel at the top of the stairs?'

Mandy nodded. 'Shall we go and explore when you've finished unpacking?' she said, putting down the bottle. After hours of sitting still on the coach, she felt like stretching her legs.

A few minutes later, they walked along the landing, past the huge oak wheel and down the staircase. James paused to look at a large print hanging at the bottom of the stairs. 'So that's what Greenwich was like three hundred years ago,' he said to Mandy, reading the caption beneath the picture. 'Look at all those ships on the Thames!'

'Aye, the river was a busy old place,' said Mac, who was just about to take the last of the suitcases upstairs. 'There's been many a king and queen of England who'd sail up river to Greenwich, and bring the whole court with them too. Henry VIII was born here, you know, and Elizabeth I used to spend the summers at Greenwich.'

Mandy glanced round the crowded hall. There were so many things to look at! Wooden seagulls, which were suspended from the ceiling, flapped their wings gracefully when she and James pulled their cords. In one corner stood a big iron-bound chest and above it were shelves crammed with what looked like old navigational instruments – a brass telescope, a compass and others Mandy couldn't identify. Shells and crystals were on display, too, and a huge shark's jawbone. Mac put down the luggage he was carrying and came over to the two friends when he noticed them looking at it.

'Did you know a shark's teeth were arranged in rows?' he said, taking the jawbone off the shelf to show it to them. 'So if the creature loses one, another grows forward from behind to take its place.'

Mandy shivered, examining the sharp, jagged teeth. 'They're vicious!' she said.

'Too right,' Mac smiled, picking up the bags and setting off upstairs again. 'Once a shark's got hold of you, you won't get away in a hurry.'

Mandy was examining a bundle of wooden walking-sticks carved with animal heads, when all of a sudden she heard a squeaky little miaow. 'Did you hear that?' she asked James, staring eagerly all around. 'I think there's a cat here somewhere!' A real animal, rather than a carved or painted one, would make The Crow's-Nest just perfect as far as she was concerned.

'There it is!' James said quietly, nudging Mandy and pointing towards a large globe in another corner. Peeping shyly out from behind it was a small tortoiseshell cat. Its tawny fur was striped with ginger, brown and black, and its large golden eyes were as round as saucers.

'I thought so!' Mandy said, dropping to her knees and smiling at the cat. She held out her hand and called in a soft, encouraging voice, 'Come on, then, puss! Come and say hello.'

The tortoiseshell gave another reedy miaow and ventured out from behind the globe. Mandy scrabbled on the rug with her fingers and the cat bounded over, pouncing on her hand and batting it with soft paws.

'Oh, isn't she lovely!' Mandy said, grinning up at James as she played with the little creature.

'How do you know it's a she?' James asked, crouching down beside Mandy.

'Tortoiseshells are nearly always female,' Mandy said, hoping she didn't sound too much of a know-all. 'We had a male tortoiseshell in the surgery the other day with fur balls, but Dad told me they are really rare.' She scratched the cat below her ears and she began to purr, pushing her head into Mandy's hand as she stroked the soft, thick fur. Then, with a wave of her tail, she wandered away across the hall to a half-open door. Looking back at them, she miaowed again.

'Looks like she wants us to follow her,' Mandy said, getting to her feet. 'Perhaps we're going to get a guided tour!'

She went after the cat into what looked like a dining-room, full of tables and chairs. The little tortoiseshell dived under one of the tables and began to play with the trailing edge of the tablecloth, rolling on to her back again and clutching the fabric fiercely with sharp claws.

'Careful!' Mandy said, disentangling the cloth. 'You'll tear it and then Mac won't be pleased.'

'Look at that, Mandy!' James said behind her, and she followed his pointing finger. Mounted on the opposite wall was a huge, painted wooden bust of a woman. She was staring into the distance with large unseeing eyes, and long dark hair streaming out behind her as though blown by some invisible wind. The name 'Daisy May' was painted in flowing golden script on the blue shawl draped round her neck.

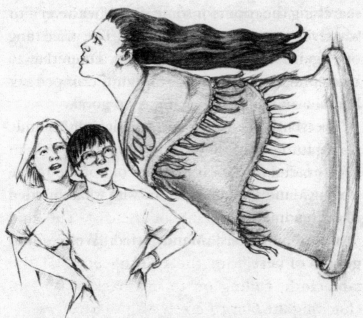

'Wow! That must be an old ship's figurehead,'
Mandy said, awestruck. 'It looks like she's bursting
through the wall and heading straight for us.
Spooky, isn't it?'

But before James could reply, there was a
sudden explosion of noise. A loud, harsh voice
came ringing through the air. 'Goodbye!' it
shouted menacingly. 'Time to go!'

'What's that?' James cried, grabbing Mandy's
arm. 'Who's there?'

'I don't know,' she replied desperately,

searching the room for some sign of whoever – or whatever – was screaming at them. The voice rang out again, even louder this time. Desperate to block out the terrifying noise, Mandy clamped her hands over her ears. But it was no good.

'Everybody's gone home!' it shrieked this time. 'Time for bed! Night-night, sleep tight!'

The tortoiseshell cat streaked out of the room, leaving Mandy and James alone with what sounded like a madman.

'Come on, James!' Mandy cried. 'We've got to get out of here!'

Three

'Look behind you!' screamed the invisible voice. Mandy and James whirled round, but there was nobody there.

'Who's that?' Mandy called as bravely as she could, beginning to feel angry now, as well as frightened. Somebody seemed to be having a joke at their expense, and it wasn't very funny.

'Daisy May is a wicked woman,' the voice said in a lower, plaintive tone.

'Wh-where are you?' James cried uncertainly. 'Come out and show yourself!'

'Have a nice day,' the voice mocked, and then

cackled. Mandy and James heard another peal of laughter behind them. They turned round to see a tall girl of about their age, with shoulder-length brown hair, watching them from the doorway with an amused look on her face.

'What's going on?' Mandy demanded, feeling slightly stupid and loosening James's grip on her arm.

'Looks like you've just met Sinbad for the first time,' the girl replied. She walked into the room and pointed towards one dark corner. There, in the shadows, stood a big cage on wheels. Inside it, a grey bird was walking delicately along the thick tree branch that served as a perch.

'So he was the one making all that noise?' Mandy said, scarcely able to believe her eyes. Her heart was still thumping madly and her palms prickled with sweat. 'Do you mean we've just been frightened half to death by a *parrot*?'

She and James went up to the birdcage for a closer look. Sinbad was slate grey, apart from his scarlet tail and the silvery white mask around his small yellow eyes. The feathers on his neck were edged in a paler shade, so that each one looked distinct and separate. Mandy thought he was just as beautiful as some of the more brightly-coloured birds she'd seen.

'Hello, Sinbad,' she said cautiously, but the parrot seemed to have decided he'd done enough talking. He stared silently at her and then sank his head down between his shoulders, ruffling up the feathers.

'He's not very friendly, is he?' James said to the girl, who'd come up to the cage beside them. 'Doesn't he like meeting strangers?'

'I asked Mac about him yesterday, when we arrived,' she replied. 'He said Sinbad's feeling very grumpy at the moment, for some reason, and it's best not to take too much notice. My name's Casey Baxter, by the way. I'm on holiday over here, from New York.'

James and Mandy introduced themselves too, and then Mandy turned back to the parrot in his cage. She couldn't help wondering why Sinbad was so hostile. 'He's a great talker,' she said to Casey. 'I wonder if we can teach him anything more friendly to say.'

'Something tells me he's not in a very friendly mood,' Casey replied.

They watched as Sinbad made his way over to

the container of seeds at the side of his cage and picked up a monkey nut with his foot. He cracked the shell with his strong curved beak and used his tongue to help take out the nut inside. James whistled the parrot a tune, but Sinbad only glared at him suspiciously.

'Let's leave him to sulk for the moment,' Casey said to them. 'Have you seen the garden yet? Come on, I'll show you.'

They said goodbye to Sinbad and left him in the quiet dining-room. 'We'll come and see you again soon,' Mandy promised, thinking the parrot looked rather forlorn as they left. She made up her mind to ask Mac all about him.

'This is such a cool place,' Casey told them as they went along a corridor to the back door. 'My dad's a doctor, and someone who works at the hospital with him visited London last year. He told us we just had to stay here.'

'Do you know why the house is so full of boats and sailing things?' Mandy asked.

'Oh, that's because Mac used to be a ship's cook,' Casey replied, opening the door on to a small courtyard garden at the back of the house. 'Just wait till you see breakfast tomorrow!' she added, walking down a cobbled path to a blue-painted bench. 'You won't need to eat again for the rest of the day, I'm telling you.'

'Have you had a look around Greenwich yet?' asked James, sitting down beside her.

'Yes, I have,' Casey said. 'We got up early this morning. There's so much to see! The park, and the Observatory, and a couple of palaces, and this wonderful ship called the Cutty Sark. It's amazing – full of figureheads like old Daisy May in the dining-room. Hey, maybe I could show it to you this afternoon? And then tomorrow we're going to see them Changing the Guard at Buckingham Palace. You'll have to come with us – if you'd like to, that is. We're going to Madame Tussaud's in the afternoon, but you have to book tickets otherwise you'll be lining up for a year, Mom says.'

'Slow down,' Mandy laughed. 'You're making me feel tired!' She gazed around the garden. To her delight, there was the tortoiseshell cat, lying in a sunny spot beneath a rosemary bush. She walked over to say hello. The cat got to her feet, arched her back, and then twined around Mandy's legs, miaowing.

'That's Patch,' Casey called over. 'She's beautiful, isn't she?'

'Lovely!' Mandy replied, picking Patch up and burying her face in the cat's soft, warm fur. She suddenly felt quite certain that they couldn't have found a nicer place to stay in the whole of London.

The next day, it was time to start sightseeing. The Hopes met Casey's parents over a huge cooked breakfast that morning, and they were soon getting on so well they decided to spend the day together.

'That's awesome!' Casey said to Mandy a few hours later as they gazed between tall iron railings at the imposing sight of Buckingham Palace stretched out in front of them. 'So this is where the Queen lives when she's in London, right? Do you think she's looking down on us at this very moment?'

'She might be,' James said. He pointed up to a red and gold flag fluttering against the blue sky. 'Look, the Royal Standard's flying. When she's not at the Palace, they put up the Union Jack instead. I was reading all about it in my guidebook last night.'

'Wow!' Casey grinned. She waved her arm towards the empty balcony. 'How d'you do, Your Majesty? This is Casey Baxter from New York, just dropping by to say hello!'

Mandy turned to watch all the people around them. Tour guides held up different coloured umbrellas so they could be seen by their groups, families posed for photographs and hot-dog sellers jostled for the best position. Mandy wrinkled her nose. The frying onions smelled delicious but, as a vegetarian, she wasn't tempted by the sausages.

All of a sudden, she spotted something she hadn't expected to see. Sitting near one of the hot-dog stands was an adorable, chocolate-brown Labrador puppy, head cocked to one side as it stared longingly up at the sausages. Mandy looked at the pup more closely, and then gazed at the people standing around it. No one seemed to be taking much notice of the little dog, but she felt sure its owner was somewhere nearby. An animal as young as that wouldn't have been left to wander around alone in the middle of London.

Casey was still engrossed in what was happening at the Palace, so Mandy nudged James.

'Look!' she said. 'There's a puppy over there, and it seems to be all on its own. Do you think it's run away from someone?'

'Oh, isn't it lovely?' James said as he spotted the cute little pup. 'You're right, though – there doesn't seem to be anybody looking after it. Is it wearing a collar?'

'I'm not sure,' Mandy said, narrowing her eyes as she stared over. 'We're too far away to tell. Come on, let's go a bit nearer and find out what's happening.'

'Where are you going? You'll lose your place!' Casey called after them from her look-out post by the railings, but James and Mandy were already hurrying off.

'We'll be back in a second,' Mandy called over her shoulder. There was no time to explain.

'I think I've got something that might help us catch the puppy if we need to,' James said, searching his jacket pockets as they threaded their way through the crowd. 'Yes! Here it is!' Triumphantly, he pulled out an ancient-looking dog biscuit. 'Left over from one of Blackie's obedience classes,' he explained.

'Great!' Mandy said, her eyes fixed on the

puppy. Some people in the crowd were glancing at it from time to time and smiling, but most of them were too busy waiting for something to happen at the Palace to pay the pup much attention.

'It's not trailing a lead,' James said as they approached. 'I don't even think it's wearing a collar.'

'And it's definitely alone,' Mandy added. 'We'd better try and catch it, in case it takes off into the traffic.' She crouched down a little way off, not wanting to frighten the young animal away, and clapped her hands on her thighs to attract its attention. 'Come on,' she called cheerfully. 'There's a good dog! Look what we've got for you!'

The pup looked up at the sound of her voice and raised its soft brown ears inquiringly. 'That's the way!' James called encouragingly, holding out the dog biscuit. 'Over here!'

The puppy gave a short bark and bounded towards them, ears pricked and tail wagging furiously at the sight – and smell – of food. 'You're hungry, aren't you?' Mandy said, as she watched it wolf down the biscuit James was offering.

'Labrador puppies are always hungry,' James

said smiling, as the pup licked his hand with a rough pink tongue. 'Do you remember what Blackie was like when he was small? He'd eat anything in sight! And this puppy looks like it's smiling at us, just like Blackie does. Do you think it's male or female?'

'Hard to tell for sure,' Mandy replied, as she watched the puppy frisking around. 'It won't keep still for long enough, but I think it's a male dog, don't you? Mum and Dad can tell us if I'm right.'

The young dog had lost his fat baby tummy, but he still had that soft, puppyish look around the face and seemed not quite able to control his long legs yet. Mandy patted his silky brown fur and the pup pushed a damp, cold nose into her hand.

'He doesn't look like a stray,' James said. 'His coat's in fantastic condition.'

Mandy stroked one of the puppy's soft ears and he gazed adoringly up at her with melting brown eyes. 'No, I think you've got a good home somewhere, haven't you?' she asked. 'And we've got to get you back there!'

The puppy gave another short bark and began to dash around them, wagging his tail furiously and crouching down on his front legs, waiting for

James and Mandy to join in the game.

'Quick, James!' Mandy cried, unbuckling the belt around her jeans so she could use it as a temporary lead. 'We have to catch him before he runs off again!'

'Let me just get a photo,' James said, already looking through the viewfinder of his camera. The puppy stared inquisitively back at him.

And then disaster struck. A mounted policewoman on a dapple-grey horse rode up to the hot-dog sellers. 'Clear this area immediately!' she said in a loud voice. 'You've been told a hundred times not to operate here. It's illegal. Go on, off you go – right now. There are horses coming and you'd better not get in the way!'

At once, everyone in the crowd surged forward, cameras at the ready, to get a good look at the Household Cavalry who were riding down past Buckingham Palace on the way back to their barracks in Hyde Park. Grumbling, the hot-dog sellers began to wheel their trolleys away through the throng. But in all the chaos, the puppy disappeared.

'Where's he gone?' Mandy cried desperately, looking around. Normally, she'd have loved to watch the mounted guards riding past on their sleek, beautifully groomed black horses. But now, all she could think about was the little animal. She couldn't bear to imagine him being trampled under the horses' hooves, or running out into the road and getting knocked over by a car. 'James, we have to find the puppy quickly!'

'I can't see him anywhere!' he shouted back, already separated from Mandy by a crush of people. 'He seems to have vanished!'

Frantically, they dropped their gaze and searched through the forest of legs around them

for any sign of the pup. But it was hopeless – there was no trace of the little dog.

'Let's go and find Mum and Dad,' Mandy called to James. 'They can help us search. Come on, there's no time to lose!'

'I don't think there's anything more we can do for now,' Emily Hope said, putting a comforting arm round Mandy's shoulders. 'I don't want you and James getting lost in the crowd as well – that won't help anybody. Let's wait until it starts to thin out, and then we'll be able to spot this puppy of yours. Why don't you go and watch with Casey for the moment?'

'OK,' Mandy said disconsolately. 'I suppose it might take our mind off things. We'll see you back here when Changing the Guard is finished.'

It took James and Mandy a while to make their way through the packed crowd of tourists. Eventually, though, they spotted Casey's baseball cap and managed to join her by the railings at the front, where the best views were to be had.

'What happened to you two?' she asked.

'We spotted this little lost puppy by a hot-dog stand,' Mandy explained miserably, 'but he ran away before we could catch him.'

'Oh, no!' Casey said, giving Mandy a sympathetic pat on the back. 'When the display is over, I'll help you search some more. Look, here come the new guards!'

A group of soldiers in scarlet and black uniforms had appeared on the Palace forecourt and were marching towards the sentry boxes. Mandy was more interested in looking at the wide pavement behind her, though, just in case she spotted a flash of brown fur or a waving tail.

Suddenly Casey grabbed her arm. 'That puppy!' she asked excitedly. 'It wasn't a chocolate brown Lab, by any chance, was it?'

'Yes, it was!' Mandy replied eagerly. 'Why? Have you seen him?'

'Looks like he's just joined up for guard duty,' Casey grinned. 'Here, pull yourself up next to me, so you can watch.'

Mandy hoisted herself up by the railings and peered through. 'I don't believe it!' she exclaimed. A few paces behind the guards was their missing puppy, walking along proudly, his tail held high.

'He must have slipped through the railings,' James said, climbing up beside the two girls.

All around them, people had begun laughing and pointing at the puppy, talking excitedly in what sounded like twenty different languages. The guards didn't seem to have noticed they had a new recruit, and the pup was careful to keep a few paces behind them. When they reached the first sentry box, the little dog quickly nipped behind it. For a few seconds there was nothing to be seen, but then a mischievous brown head peeped round the corner. The soldiers were so intent on changing over guard duty that none of them spotted it. Everyone else had, though, and a loud gale of laughter rose up in the air.

'Naughty little thing!' Mandy smiled. 'He obviously thinks it's a wonderful game.'

Excited by the noise, the puppy decided he had had enough of marching and began to twirl around, chasing his tail. Then he bounded off through an archway that led to a courtyard within the Palace and disappeared from sight. There was a loud round of applause from the crowd.

'Well!' said James, chuckling. 'At least now we know he's safely away from the road.'

'I suppose so,' Mandy said doubtfully. 'I just hope he'll be OK in there.' She stared up at the long rows of windows, imagining the vast number of rooms inside the Palace, and frowned. The little dog might have found his way in, but would he ever manage to find a way out again?

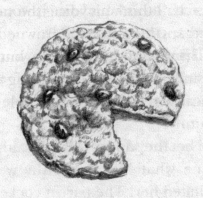

Four

The next morning, Mandy was the first person down to the dining-room. Mac was apparently in the middle of laying the breakfast tables, but he had stopped for a moment by the birdcage.

'Morning!' Mandy said, going over to join him. 'How's Sinbad today?'

'He's calmed down a bit since yesterday,' said Mac, turning away and starting to put out the cereal bowls. 'I'm sorry he gave you such a fright. Casey told me all about it last night.'

'That's OK,' Mandy replied, watching Sinbad flex his long toes and walk delicately along the wooden perch. 'I think his voice is wonderful. I've never heard anything like it!'

'I wish all my guests agreed with you,' Mac told her with a smile. 'Sinbad's an amazing mimic, like lots of African Greys, but some people don't find him very funny.'

'Oh no, I bet they don't,' Mandy said. She could just imagine what Mrs Ponsonby would say if Sinbad imitated her! The parrot cocked his head coyly and looked sideways at her out of one yellow eye. 'He does seem happier today,' she went on, watching as Sinbad began to preen his soft grey feathers carefully. 'Do you think he'd let me take him out of the cage?'

'A couple of months ago, I'd have said yes straightaway.' Mac sighed, folding a napkin. 'But now I think it would be better not to risk it. He might take a swipe at you, and that beak is very sharp!' He finished with the pile of linen and then took some grapes from a bowl on the sideboard. 'Here, why don't I take him out and you can give him some fruit?' he suggested. 'If you'd like to, that is. You seem very interested in him.'

'Oh, I am!' Mandy replied. 'My parents are vets and that's what I'd like to be too, if I can get the right grades. I've never met an African Grey before.'

'They're very intelligent birds,' Mac said, passing her the grapes and opening the cage door. 'They can be nervous, but I've had Sinbad since he was a chick and tamed him myself.' He stretched his hand into the cage and Sinbad hopped on to his finger, chirping and whistling excitedly.

'I think he's beautiful,' Mandy said, enjoying a good look at Sinbad out in the open. He watched Mac, turning his head this way and that, and seemed to listen intently as his owner talked to him. 'He has so many different expressions, doesn't he?' Mandy went on, offering the parrot a grape. 'Like he's thinking all the time.'

'You're right,' Mac agreed. 'And you should see him when he's about to sing! He ruffles up his neck feathers and looks very grand, like he's some famous Italian tenor!' They both laughed, and watched as Sinbad carefully took the grape with one claw and raised it to his beak to nibble. 'He doesn't sing much these days, though,' Mac added quietly.

'Do you know why he's so miserable at the

moment?' Mandy asked. She couldn't hear about an unhappy animal without wanting to help.

Mac shook his head. 'I don't know what's got into him,' he said anxiously. 'I've taken him to the vet for a check-up, but there isn't anything physically wrong. He just doesn't seem himself at all – he's so moody! He won't talk half as much as he used to, and when he does, he can be very aggressive – like he was with you yesterday. But the worst thing is, he's started pulling out his feathers. Look, just there.'

'Oh, yes, so he has!' Mandy said. Several of the overlapping dark grey feathers on Sinbad's breast were missing, revealing the fluffy white down beneath. 'Why would he do that?' she asked.

Mac frowned. 'I've got no idea,' he answered, putting Sinbad carefully back into the cage and shutting the door. 'I make sure he doesn't have mites and I spray him with water so his skin doesn't get too dry. I wish he'd stop, though. The vet told me it's a habit that can quickly get out of control – some birds pluck their skin bare.'

'Oh, how horrible!' Mandy exclaimed. It was awful to think of Sinbad deliberately hurting himself. He obviously had lots of love and attention, so why should he need to do such a thing? 'I'll ask Mum and Dad if there's anything we can do,' she told Mac. 'I'm sure they'll come up with something.'

Mandy didn't get a chance to talk to her mother about Sinbad until later that morning, when they were sitting on a boat together, sailing down the Thames. Mandy's gran had suggested at breakfast that a trip down the river from Greenwich to Westminster would be a good way of seeing the sights. It was a lovely sunny morning, and everyone thought going out on the water was a wonderful idea. Walter and Ernie had met up with them at Greenwich Pier, which was just around the corner from the pub where they were staying, and Casey and her parents had come along too. Dr and Mrs Baxter were getting on so well with the Hopes that it seemed natural for them all to go sightseeing together again.

Mrs Hope was not too encouraging about Sinbad's prospects. 'Feather plucking can turn into a serious problem very quickly,' she said gravely. 'There could be any number of explanations. Sinbad's skin might be irritated, or he might be under some kind of stress, or bored, or even ready for a mate. I'm happy to have a look at him, but often there's no physical reason for that kind of behaviour. You have to get to know the bird to find out why he's doing it.'

'Well then, maybe that's what we should do,' James said. Mandy had told him all about Sinbad's problem, and he'd been listening in on the conversation with her mum. 'Between us, we should be able to help him before we have to go back home.'

'I don't know,' Mrs Hope said, smiling at them both. 'First puppies, now parrots! I thought we'd left all our patients back in Welford! Just don't let worrying about Sinbad spoil your holiday.'

'We'll try not to,' Mandy promised. If there was an animal somewhere in need of help, though, she and James wouldn't rest until they'd found a solution. And Mandy's mum was just the same, no matter what she might say.

'Look – straight ahead!' James said suddenly, focusing his binoculars on the river. 'That was a cormorant, wasn't it?'

'You're right,' Mr Hope said from his seat a little further up the boat. 'There's another one sitting on that post over there. See how it holds its wings outstretched to dry them?'

'Here, have a look through these for a minute,' James said to Mandy, passing her the binoculars.

'Thanks, James,' Mandy replied, peering through them at the dark bird zigzagging down the river in front of them. Suddenly it dipped down to the water and flew back up with a flash of silver in its beak. 'Oh, it's caught something!' she exclaimed, before handing the binoculars on to Casey so she could see too.

'There's all kinds of fish coming back to the Thames now the water's so much cleaner,' the riverboat captain told them, leaning out of his cabin. 'You can even catch a salmon if you're lucky.'

The recorded commentary crackled into life to tell everyone the boat was approaching Tower Bridge, and that the Tower of London would soon be in full view on their right. They should look out for Traitors' Gate, where condemned prisoners were brought into the Tower by boat from the courts at Westminster. This would have

been the last glimpse of the outside world, for
most of them.

'I can't wait to look round the Tower,' Casey
said, as they sailed past the grim, forbidding
building. 'That's where the Crown Jewels are,
right? And the execution block where they
beheaded one of Henry VIII's wives?'

Mandy shivered – it all sounded very gloomy to
her. As far as she was concerned, it was much more
fun to be out in the sunshine on the river.

'That's right. We're going right down as far as
Westminster Pier now, but we can stop off on
the way back,' Mr Hope promised. 'After we've
taken a look at Big Ben and Westminster Abbey.
And maybe had a quick pizza,' he added
hopefully.

'Dad!' Mandy said, outraged. 'On top of that
huge breakfast? You'll have to go back on a diet
when this holiday's over!'

'I've never eaten a pizza in my life, and I don't
intend to start now,' Ernie declared. 'A sandwich
in the park will suit Walter and me, thank you very
much. There was a brass band playing there
yesterday lunch-time. Not as good as some I've
heard up North, mind you.'

'But think what Mrs Ponsonby would say, if she heard you'd had pizza for lunch!' James said innocently. 'She couldn't call you set in your ways then, could she, Mr Bell?' He caught Mandy's eye and she had to bite her lip hard to stop herself from smiling.

Ernie thought for a while. 'Maybe not,' he said eventually. 'I shall have to see how I feel.'

'Speaking of Mrs Ponsonby,' Mandy's gran broke in, 'she rang up The Crow's-Nest last night. I think she's rather lonely in that smart hotel of hers. Anyway, she's invited us all to lunch tomorrow.'

'But we're going to look round the Royal Mews tomorrow!' Mandy protested. 'Dad promised he'd take us.' On their way back from Buckingham Palace the day before, James had spotted a sign for the Royal Mews, 'the largest working stable in London'. It was closed at the weekend, but Mandy, James and Casey all wanted to go back there on Monday. A chance to see the Queen's magnificent carriage horses close up was just too good to miss. And besides, they might be able to ask someone if a Labrador puppy had been found anywhere in the Palace. Mandy was counting on that!

'Don't worry,' her grandmother reassured her. 'I suggested we should all meet up for a picnic in St James's Park. It's just opposite the Palace, so you won't have to miss out on anything.'

'And we can take Pandora for a walk,' James said. 'I bet Mrs Ponsonby hasn't been exercising her properly.'

'Oh, James, that's a great idea,' Mandy said, beaming at him. 'Who knows, we might even get Dad to go jogging!'

'Mum, Dad, after we've seen Westminster Abbey, do you think we could go to the viewing tower in Westminster Cathedral?' Mandy asked, looking up from James's guide book. They were all standing beside Big Ben, waiting for James to finish trying to photograph the clock face. 'It's in Victoria Street, where the shops are,' she went on, 'so I'm sure there'll be a restaurant near by.'

'Well, OK, as long as the Baxters are happy with that,' Mr Hope replied. 'I didn't realise you were so keen on sightseeing, love.'

On their way over to the cathedral, Mandy explained her plan to James and Casey. 'According to James's book, you can see right into the gardens at Buckingham Palace from the top of the tower,' she said as they walked along the empty Sunday-morning street. 'I know it's a long shot, but if we can get a good view . . .'

'. . . We might be able to spot that Labrador puppy we saw yesterday,' James finished off for her, slinging the binoculars round his neck.

'Exactly!' Mandy said. She knew that James wouldn't have forgotten the little dog either. The puppy had probably been found by now, but there was a slim chance it might still be running round the Palace grounds. Perhaps if they spotted it, they could alert one of the police officers by the gate. At the very least, it would be good to see the pup again and make sure it was safe.

They soon reached the cathedral, set back from the road with a large paved area in front. Mrs Hope put her finger to her lips as they went through the huge doors, because there was a church service going on. They made their way quietly to the lift that would take them up to the viewing platform.

'Well, that's a real English lift,' Dr Baxter said as its doors opened. 'It's half the size of our elevators! We won't all fit in.'

'Why don't I take the young 'uns up first?' the attendant suggested. 'It's quite safe at the top – you can't fall out.'

'Good idea!' Mandy said at once. She knew her mother felt she should stop worrying about animals and just enjoy the holiday, so it would be much better if they had a few minutes on their own to look for the pup.

The view from the top of the tower might have been spectacular, but it was a big disappointment as far as they were concerned. 'Maybe you could see into the Palace gardens ten years ago,' James said, squinting through his binoculars, 'but you certainly can't now. There's a great big office block in the way!'

Mandy sighed as she looked towards Buckingham Palace. She could just see the golden top of the Victoria monument outside its gates and the green trees in St James's Park, but that was about it. There was no way they could look into the gardens, even with binoculars. And then, suddenly, a flurry of activity beneath them caught her eye. Some tourists were milling about in the square below, while a small shape ran to and fro around their group. A small brown shape . . .

'James! Casey! Look down there, where those people are,' she cried excitedly. 'I think it might be the puppy!'

'Where?' Casey demanded, squeezing in beside her and peering down. 'I can't see where you mean. Hang on a minute . . . ! Yes! You're right – that's him!'

'Looks like he's playing with somebody,' James added over her shoulder. 'Or maybe chasing a pigeon.'

'Well then, what are we waiting for? Come on, let's see if we can get him!' Mandy cried, already rushing out. 'Quick, before he runs off again!'

Casey's parents and the Hopes were just getting out of the lift as Mandy, James and Casey arrived to take it back down. 'We've had a good look,' Mandy told her parents quickly as the three of them squeezed into the lift. 'See you downstairs, outside the cathedral.'

'What's going on?' Mrs Baxter asked. 'Why are you in such a hurry?'

'We'll explain later,' Casey promised as the lift doors closed and the surprised attendant started taking them back to ground level.

'Come on, lift,' Mandy groaned as they creaked

slowly downwards. 'Hurry up! I couldn't bear it if we lost the puppy again. We're so close now!'

Eventually the doors opened. They walked through the quiet cathedral as quickly as they could without running, and then out into the square. 'Oh no!' James cried in dismay. 'Where's he gone?' The group of tourists were scattering towards the street, and there was no sign of the little dog anywhere among them.

'We're looking for the puppy that was here just now,' Mandy said to a large man in sunglasses at the back of the group. 'Did you see where he went?' But he just smiled and waved at her, obviously not understanding a word.

'There he is!' Casey shouted suddenly. 'Look, down that little back road!' She rushed across the square and then stepped out to cross the side road – straight into the path of a black London taxi. There was a horrible squeal of brakes, followed by the even more terrifying noise of a heavy thud as Casey's body hit the front of the cab.

'Casey!' Mandy screamed, running towards her. 'James, go back and get Dr Baxter – and hurry!'

Five

Mandy flew across the pavement towards Casey, her heart pounding and her eyes fixed on the slumped body. Casey had been thrown back by the force of the collision, and was now lying, terrifyingly still, on the pavement. As Mandy approached, though, she saw Casey begin to struggle up on one elbow.

'No! Stop!' she cried, kneeling beside her. 'Just stay here – don't try to get up.' She knew from experience with animals who'd been run over that a patient shouldn't be moved before getting medical attention. That could do further damage to broken bones or back injuries.

The taxi driver came rushing over to join them, his face as pale as Casey's. 'Is she all right?' he asked desperately. 'Tell me she's not badly hurt!'

'I don't think so,' Mandy said, quickly taking off her jacket and folding it into a pillow which she tucked under Casey's head. Casey was as white as a sheet and trembling a little, but her breathing was regular and her skin wasn't cold and clammy. As far as Mandy could tell, she wasn't in serious shock.

'What happened?' she asked in a dazed voice.

'You had an argument with a London taxi,' Mandy said, as calmly as she could, smoothing the hair back from Casey's face. 'I think the taxi won. Just lie still for now. Everything's going to be fine, don't you worry.'

'Why won't you let me get up off the sidewalk?' Casey asked feebly. 'I feel like an idiot lying here.' A small crowd was gathering around them by now. People were craning curiously to see who had been knocked over and if the victim was badly hurt.

'I think we should wait till your parents arrive,' Mandy said, pushing up the sleeve of Casey's sweatshirt so she could check her pulse wasn't racing too fast. 'James has gone to fetch them, so your dad'll be here any minute. He's a doctor,' she added, for the taxi driver's benefit.

'Well, I can see she's in good hands,' he replied thankfully, wiping a shaking hand across his forehead. 'Thanks, love. There was nothing I could do! She just stepped out in front of me!'

By now the Baxters were racing towards them, with James and the Hopes not far behind. Dr Baxter pushed his way through to Casey, then crouched down and began running his hands expertly over her body, talking to her all the while in a calm, gentle voice. Casey's mum knelt at her daughter's head, stroking her hair and trying very hard not to cry.

Quietly, Mandy stepped away. She'd done all she could, and she felt the Baxters needed some privacy. Her father obviously agreed, for he began to clear all the onlookers away. In a firm but pleasant voice, he asked everyone to give the family some space, telling them that everything was under control.

'Well done, love,' Mandy's mum said, giving her a comforting hug. 'Looks like you've done exactly the right thing.'

'Do you think she'll be OK?' James asked anxiously. Mandy nodded, not trusting herself to speak. She'd been fine when there was something to do, but now the shock of the accident was beginning to hit her. And then she remembered why Casey had been rushing across the street in the first place. The puppy! She looked over towards the side street, but it seemed deserted.

James followed her gaze. 'I'll go and take a quick look,' he said quietly. 'As long as there's nothing else I can do . . .'

'I think Casey's parents are the best people to look after her now,' Mandy said. 'Thanks, James.'

At last Dr Baxter began to help Casey up. 'She's fine, amazingly enough,' he said, when Casey was back on her feet, looking rather unsteady. 'No broken bones, and no internal injuries either – just a big shock to the system.'

Mandy let out her breath in relief, and everyone broke into smiles.

'Thank God!' said the taxi driver. 'I'm so sorry! She stepped right out in front of me,' he repeated to Casey's parents. 'Maybe she's not used to the traffic?'

'Hey! I live in New York,' Casey told him in a shaky voice. 'Of course I'm used to traffic! I'm just not used to it coming at me from the wrong direction, that's all.'

'We're going to get a nice hot cup of English tea, and then go straight back to Greenwich,' said Mrs Baxter, blowing her nose on a tissue. 'I think we've had enough excitement for one day.'

'I'll catch you later,' Casey said to Mandy as she was led away. 'We'll have a talk about you know what!'

Just then, Mandy saw James hurrying back

towards her. She raised her eyebrows at him in a silent question, although she could already tell from his disappointed expression that he had nothing to report. He just shook his head.

'And now I think we need a little chat, don't you?' Mandy's mother asked them both sternly. 'What were the three of you up to? Why was Casey running across the road like that?'

Mandy and James looked at each other, and then down at the ground. 'We spotted the puppy again when we were up in the tower,' Mandy said eventually. 'Casey saw it go down that side street, but now it's run off somewhere else.'

Mrs Hope sighed. 'Didn't you remember what I told you this morning?' she asked Mandy, a serious look in her green eyes. 'Look, of course we have to help an animal in trouble, but this puppy search seems to be turning into a wild-goose chase – and a dangerous one at that. Casey could have been killed just now!'

'London is a huge place,' Mr Hope added firmly. 'We can't possibly spend our whole holiday searching for a puppy that could be anywhere by now. It'd be like looking for a needle in a haystack! Somebody will find him and take him in to the police, I'm sure of it. So no more running around after lost dogs, OK? And certainly not now – it's time for lunch!'

'OK,' said Mandy, realising that she had to accept what her parents said – for the time being, at least. Inside her head, though, she made the puppy a silent promise. *Don't worry, we won't forget about you. We'll keep looking, if we can!*

When Mandy, James and her parents got back to The Crow's-Nest later that afternoon, Mac told them that Casey was resting in her room. The next morning, when the Baxters came down to breakfast, Mandy noticed Casey was walking a little stiffly. 'How are you?' she asked her straightaway. 'We've been so worried!'

'Oh, I really am fine,' Casey said. 'Just feeling a bit stupid for causing all this fuss and bother. And I have a bruise on my butt the size of a dinner plate.' She sat down next to Mandy and James, whose face had turned beetroot red. 'I don't suppose you saw any sign of the pup after all that commotion, did you?' she asked.

'No. I went down the side street to look, but he'd disappeared,' James replied, unfolding his napkin and trying to pretend he wasn't really blushing at all.

Mandy took a quick glance at her parents, sitting at the next table, and saw they were already chatting away to Dr and Mrs Baxter. 'Mum and Dad told us we should forget about the puppy for now,' she told Casey, lowering her voice. 'But I can't bear to think of him running around those busy streets. I wish he'd stayed in the Palace – he'd have been safer there.'

'I'm sure someone will catch him soon,' Casey said comfortingly, helping herself to orange juice from a big jug. 'He can't stay on the loose for ever.'

'Just so long as he doesn't get knocked over first,' Mandy worried, holding out her glass so Casey could fill it too. 'And what's he finding to eat? Where's he sleeping at night?'

'I bet he'll have found someone to look after him by now,' James answered reassuringly as he tucked into a bowlful of cereal. 'He's such a friendly little thing. Anyway, we'll be able to keep our eyes open for any sign of him when we go to the Royal Mews this morning. You are coming, aren't you, Casey?'

' 'fraid not,' Casey said. 'I'm still under house arrest. Dad says I've got to have a couple more quiet days before he'll let me back into the city.'

So after breakfast, they said goodbye to Casey and set off for the Royal Mews. Dorothy Hope, Mrs McFarlane and Eileen Davy were going to meet up with them at lunch-time in St James's Park, bringing a picnic Mac had prepared. 'Though I'm not sure a picnic will be grand enough for Mrs Ponsonby,' Mandy's gran told her. 'After a weekend in that wonderful hotel of hers, she's probably not prepared to sit on a rug in the park!'

Mandy stared up and down the street as she walked with James and her parents towards the Royal Mews at the side of Buckingham Palace. It was really no distance from where they'd been the day before – just a couple of roads away from Westminster Cathedral. But what busy roads they were! Mandy felt her heart sink as she watched the speeding traffic and the hundreds of people hurrying along the pavement. How could any puppy find its way safely around such a noisy, terrifying city?

'Wait till we get inside the stables,' James said

quietly to her. 'We may get a chance to ask if anyone spotted a puppy yesterday.'

It was a disappointing morning, though, as far as lost Labradors were concerned. Mandy and James both loved seeing the beautiful carriage horses, but none of the attendants had any news of a puppy having been reported around the Palace the day before. The stables were at the side of Buckingham Palace and backed on to the Palace grounds, so they kept their eyes open as they walked round. If the pup was still there, though, he didn't seem to want to be found.

After a couple of hours at the Royal Mews, they crossed the wide roads in front of the Palace and entered St James's Park to meet the others for lunch. Mandy began to feel more cheerful as she looked at the view. There was a lake in the middle of the park, sparkling in the sun, with a pretty bridge across it. Ducks and a couple of majestic swans were swimming to and fro underneath.

'It's like being back in the country!' she said to James.

'According to my guidebook there used to be a herd of cows kept here,' James replied. 'They'd milk them on the spot if anyone was thirsty, and charge a penny a glass. That was about three hundred years ago, though.'

Emily Hope laughed. 'What would we do without you and your guidebook, James!' she said, putting an arm round his shoulders and making him blush again.

As they headed across the grass towards the bandstand where they'd arranged to meet the others, Mandy heard a familiar voice booming out.

'I told the hotel manager that Pandora was extremely well-behaved,' Mrs Ponsonby was saying. 'After all, I trained her myself! There is no reason why she shouldn't be allowed into the dining-room. If anyone wants to complain, I'll soon put them right!'

Mrs Ponsonby was sitting in a deckchair next to Mandy's gran, in the shade of some trees near the bandstand. Miss Davy and Mrs McFarlane were with them too, helping to lay out Mac's picnic on a checked rug. Pandora was sitting on Mrs Ponsonby's lap, staring at the food and drooling.

'Hello, everyone,' Mandy said, dropping to her knees on the rug and suddenly realising she was starving. 'This picnic looks great!'

'Oh, hello, love!' her gran said, taking some cartons of juice out of the bag. She looked very relieved to see them. 'Have you had a good morning? I've been wondering when you were all going to get here.'

'Hello there, Mandy and James! And the rest of the family too, I see,' Mrs Ponsonby said, waving and smiling in a gracious manner. 'So nice to see familiar faces in the middle of London. Of course, when I meet the Queen, her face will look very familiar! But that's not quite the same, is it?' She laughed loudly.

Mandy passed round the paper plates and helped herself to an egg roll. She sat back on the rug, enjoying the fresh air and the warmth of the sun on her skin, listening to the others chatting quietly together. Gradually, though, she became aware of a strange snuffling sound above the background murmur. Pandora had jumped down from Mrs Ponsonby's lap and was advancing steadily towards some sausages, her little pink tongue hanging out of her mouth.

'Uh-oh, Pandora's decided it's time for her lunch too,' Mandy said, moving the plate to a corner of the rug out of the Peke's reach. She gave her a quick pat to make sure there were no hard feelings. Pandora shuffled back to her mistress's deckchair, looking rather put out.

'Never mind, my precious,' Mrs Ponsonby cooed, scooping her up again. 'You shall have some lovely chicken from Mummy's plate in a minute.'

Mandy and James exchanged glances. 'No wonder Pandora wants to eat our picnic,' Mandy whispered to James. 'You'd think Mrs Ponsonby would know better than to feed her like that.'

'So what have the rest of you been up to whilst we've been inspecting the Queen's horses?' her father said, munching on a cheese and tomato sandwich.

'We spent a most enjoyable morning at the Maritime Museum,' Miss Davy said. 'It was very interesting, and the staff were charming. Mr Pickard and Mr Bell came too.'

Suddenly Mandy froze, her roll halfway to her mouth. 'James!' she hissed. 'James! Look over there! And keep quiet!'

James had been about to pop open a packet of crisps. He put them down and stared around, trying to work out where Mandy was looking. And then his eyes widened as he caught sight of what she'd seen. From behind the large plane tree they were sitting under, an inquisitive little head was peeping out. A chocolate brown head, with soft floppy ears and shining dark eyes.

'There he is!' Mandy whispered excitedly, sitting up on her heels. 'That's our puppy!'

Six

As soon as he realised he'd been spotted, the little dog hid behind the tree again. Mandy held her breath, then released it slowly as she saw the Labrador's appealing face come back into view. Just like Pandora, he was staring hungrily at the sausages. Without realising it, Mandy had brought the plate much closer to him when she'd moved it away from the Pekinese.

'We've got to take this slowly,' she whispered to James. 'He seems much more jumpy now than when we saw him at the Palace.'

As casually as possible, she moved the plate of

sausages almost within the puppy's reach, in order to tempt him out. Trying not to startle him, she watched out of the corner of her eye as the little dog put his head on one side and licked his lips hungrily. He looked quite thin now, and there were muddy patches on his bedraggled brown coat. The puppy must have been having quite a tough time, and Mandy felt her heart melt. They had to make sure he was safe and properly looked after.

But she had forgotten Pandora. The Peke had obviously decided those sausages belonged to her, and she was watching them jealously. Growling softly in her throat, she waddled forward over the rug in hot pursuit of her escaping dinner. Unfortunately, the pup had chosen this very moment to pluck up his courage to dash out from the safety of the tree. He and Pandora came face to face with each other. The young Labrador was already taller than the fat little Pekinese, but there was no doubt who was top dog. Pandora bristled, her silky cream coat quivering with fury like an indignant powder puff, and let out a stream of shrill yaps.

'Pandora! My precious!' Mrs Ponsonby shrieked

in alarm, struggling up from her deckchair to find out what was the matter.

It was all too much for the poor Labrador puppy. He turned tail and fled across the grass towards the bandstand.

Mandy was already on her feet. 'Come on, James!' she called, tearing off after the puppy. 'We can't let him get away!'

Now that the pup was almost within their grasp, she was determined not to lose him again. She didn't want to alarm him even more by the chase, but they had to stop him once and for all. It was too dangerous for him to go running around on his own.

And then her eyes widened in horror. 'James!' she called, gasping for breath. 'Look where he's heading!'

The puppy was making straight for the huge ornamental gates at the side of the park, which lay wide open. Beyond them, traffic was speeding along the busy road and, if they weren't careful, they could drive the puppy straight into the path of the oncoming cars.

James waved and Mandy knew he'd seen the danger. He veered around in a circle to the left so that the puppy wouldn't be frightened by someone running just behind him. Then he swung back to try and head the puppy off before he could reach the gate. It was hopeless, though. The dog was too fast and they were both running out of steam – they just couldn't reach him in time.

Mandy could hardly bear to look as the pup headed straight for the inviting, open gates in front of him. A couple of people were strolling casually past, and Mandy yelled, 'Stop the puppy! Please, somebody, stop him!' But no one seemed to hear.

And then, just as the little Labrador was about to dash through the gates, a large group of tourists appeared. They stood in a long line along the pavement with their backs to the park, chatting excitedly and taking photographs of Buckingham Palace.

'Oh, thank goodness!' Mandy gasped to herself. The gateway was blocked.

The Labrador skidded as he turned around in confusion, all long legs and over-sized paws, and stood there, panting.

Mandy put on a final burst of speed. 'Got you!' she gasped, flinging her arms round the puppy and holding his heaving, wriggling body tight to her chest.

'Well, he's not in too bad shape, considering he's been on the run for a few days,' Adam Hope said, straightening up after examining the pup and giving him a pat on the head. 'And he *is* a he, too, if you see what I mean.'

'Are you sure he's OK?' Mandy said. She could detect a note of hesitation in her father's voice. 'Is anything wrong?'

'Well, I'm just a bit worried about his right ear,' Adam Hope replied. 'Do you see how he keeps shaking his head? And there's a lot of wax there. I think he might have some kind of irritation inside.'

'A grass seed perhaps?' Emily Hope said, looking over his shoulder. 'Difficult to tell without an auriscope, isn't it?'

'Is that serious?' Mandy asked, looking intently at the puppy.

'It could be,' her father replied. 'Grass seeds work their way down the dog's ear canal, you see, because of their pointed shape. If they end up next to the eardrum they can cause a lot of pain

or discomfort. We really need to get him to a vet right away so that ear can be properly examined with an auriscope, like your mother says.'

'Poor little thing.' Mandy said, stroking the pup gently. He was still quite wary but seemed much less frightened now, and lifted his head at the sound of her voice to lick her chin. 'What will happen to him if there is something stuck in his ear?' she asked.

'He'll have to have a general anaesthetic if there is an obstruction,' Mrs Hope replied. 'Just to keep him still while it's taken out.'

'But how do we know where the nearest vet is?' James asked anxiously. 'And what will happen to him after that?'

'Well, we could ring the RSPCA,' Adam Hope suggested. 'They'll probably treat him and then take him to a centre for stray dogs. They'll be able to find out there if he's been microchipped.'

'Oh, I hope he has,' Mandy said. She knew how much easier it was to reunite dogs with their owners if they'd had a specially coded microchip put into the scruff of their neck.

'Poor thing,' Mandy's gran said kindly, looking

at the timid little dog. 'It will all seem very strange to him.'

'Couldn't we just take him to the dogs' home ourselves?' Mandy asked her father. 'I'm sure they'll have a vet who could look at his ear. He's already becoming used to us, and it would be much less unsettling for him.'

'Do you know, I've always wanted to visit a dogs' home!' Eileen Davy said enthusiastically. 'Ever since I saw a television programme about one. May I come along with you?'

'All right, all right!' Mr Hope said, raising his hands in surrender. 'I can see when I'm outnumbered. Why don't the four of us take the pup in? I'm sure a taxi driver would know where the dogs' home is. Then your mother can have a nice long shop this afternoon with Gran.'

'I've got your number, Adam Hope!' Emily laughed. 'You'd do anything to get out of a shopping trip . . .'

'Casey's going to be so cross that she missed out on this,' Mandy said, as she sat with James and Miss Davy in the back of a black London taxi on their way to the dogs' home. The puppy dozed on the seat between them, his head resting on his paws. Occasionally he whimpered, and scratched his ear with his paw.

'We'll have to tell her all about it,' James said, stroking the puppy comfortingly. 'By the way, what do you think about Brownie as a name for the puppy?' he went on. 'Only for the moment, of course. He just reminds me so much of Blackie when he was little.'

'Hmm, maybe.' Mandy looked at the Labrador pup and tried to think of a way not to hurt James's feelings. 'Blackie is the perfect name for Blackie, of course. But I'm not quite so sure about Brownie . . .'

'Well, what about Bruno?' Miss Davy suggested. 'Would you say that had more of a ring to it?'

'Perfect!' James and Mandy decided together.

'Now don't go getting too attached to this puppy,' Adam Hope said, smiling at them from the pull-down seat opposite. 'We're taking him to the dogs' home and leaving him there so that his owner can claim him. And we're not bringing any other strays back with us to Welford, Mandy, no matter how appealing they are.'

'Don't worry, Dad,' Mandy sighed. 'I know the

rule.' There were too many animal patients at the Ark for the Hopes to adopt any more as pets. Mandy understood that, even though it was hard to accept sometimes.

The taxi soon drew up outside the dogs' home. Mr Hope paid the driver while James carried Bruno inside, holding him tightly, and Mandy followed on with Miss Davy. The puppy looked round nervously, trembling a little at the roar of the traffic.

'He's so much jumpier now than he was when we first saw him,' Mandy commented to Miss Davy. She'd already told her all about their first sighting of the pup at Buckingham Palace. 'It makes you wonder what's been happening to him over the past couple of days.'

'The poor creature must be terrified,' Miss Davy said sympathetically, holding an inner door open so James could carry Bruno into the reception area.

Ten minutes later, they were all sitting in a side room with Penny, who took charge of the dogs that people brought in. The door was firmly shut and Penny was giving the chocolate brown Labrador time to sniff around and get the feel of the place while she asked Mandy and James how they'd found him. They told her all about it, and Mr Hope told her about the puppy's ear problem too.

'I'll get Frank to have a look at him right away,' Penny said, completing the registration form.

After she had spoken to the centre's vet on the phone, she gazed thoughtfully at the puppy with her calm grey eyes. 'It certainly looks like he's come from a good home,' she commented. 'But I checked the register earlier this morning and I don't remember anyone having reported a missing Labrador. I'd have thought his owner would have been on to us or the police by now. Let me just check if he's been microchipped.' She ran a scanner over the scruff of Bruno's neck. 'No, nothing, I'm afraid,' she said, shaking her head.

'What if his owner never gets in touch?' James asked. 'What will happen to him then?'

'We'll keep him for seven days in the holding kennel,' Penny replied, taking a collar with a numbered identification disc and buckling it round Bruno's neck. 'If his owner hasn't turned up to claim him by then, he'll be moved over to the sale block so we can find him a new home.'

'Oh, Bruno!' Mandy said, unable to resist giving him another cuddle. 'How could anybody bear to part with you?'

'Don't worry,' Penny smiled. 'We'll take good care of him. If he isn't claimed, we'll make sure he goes to a new family who'll look after him properly. He won't be with us for long, I'm sure.' She snapped a lead on to the puppy's collar and stood up. 'Now then, Bruno, are you going to show me how well you walk to heel? Let's go and find your kennel! Then our vet can come and have a look at you. He's on his rounds now.'

'May we come too?' Mandy asked. 'Just to make sure he's OK?' She'd formed a real bond with this little puppy from the moment she'd first set eyes on him, and she was sure James felt the same. Saying goodbye was going to be very hard.

'Of course,' Penny said, looking at their sad faces. 'Why don't you all come, and then afterwards I can show you some of the other dogs? We've got cats too, though you might not have realised. They're much quieter!'

'That sounds like a good idea,' Adam Hope replied, putting a comforting arm round Mandy's shoulders. 'Let's go and see Bruno's new apartment!'

As they approached the kennel block, Mandy could hear the sound of barking. It rose to a crescendo when Penny opened the door and showed them in to a room lined on both sides with cages. They held about fifty dogs of all shapes and sizes. Some crowded up against the wire, yapping fit to burst, while others stayed in their baskets, looking out silently with nervous eyes. Bruno shrank back from the noise, so Penny scooped him up and carried him as she walked towards an empty kennel.

'These are the dogs that have been brought in today,' she said to James and Mandy over the din, pointing to the cages along one side of the room. 'The summer is our busiest time, I'm afraid. Some people don't bother to make proper arrangements for their pets when they go on holiday. They just turn them out on the street to fend for themselves.'

'They shouldn't be allowed to keep animals ever again,' Mandy said fiercely. Cruelty like that was something she would never understand or forgive. It made her blood boil.

Bruno was beginning to struggle in Penny's arms, so she handed him to Mandy and said, 'Would you like to put him in his basket? I think he's more used to you than he is to me.' She opened the door of the cage and stood back to let Mandy and James take Bruno inside. 'Don't worry, the vet will be here any minute,' she added reassuringly.

'We'll wait here,' Mr Hope said, as he and Miss Davy looked on. 'We don't want to crowd him.'

Mandy carefully settled the puppy into his basket. James knelt down beside her, giving Bruno a farewell pat before taking one last photograph for his collection.

'There you are, Bruno,' Mandy said encouragingly, arranging his blanket comfortably and trying to swallow the lump in her throat. She kissed the top of his satin-smooth head and whispered, 'It was nice knowing you. Goodbye, and good luck!'

Seven

'Now come on, you two,' Adam Hope said to James and Mandy, clapping an arm round each of their shoulders. 'There's no need to be upset. I bet Bruno's owner will come and collect him soon. He's in exactly the right place, and you've done the best for him you possibly could. So cheer up!'

'That's right,' Miss Davy added. 'And remember what Penny's told you – even if his owner doesn't turn up, there'll be plenty of people wanting to give Bruno a good home.'

'I suppose so,' Mandy said, blinking away her

tears. 'It's just strange leaving him here without knowing what's going to happen.'

'Well, you can always give me a ring in a few days' time to see if there's any news,' Penny said, leading them back out of the room. 'I'm sure we'll be able to rehome Bruno very quickly if we have to. Everyone wants a puppy, especially a pure-bred. It's a pity, really. So many of our older mongrels make brilliant family pets. Training an excitable puppy takes lots more time and patience.'

'That's true,' James said, and Mandy could tell exactly whom he was thinking of. 'I've got a black Labrador at home and he doesn't always do as he's told, even now he's fully grown!'

Penny took them over to what she called the 'sale block'. 'These are the dogs that are waiting to be rehomed,' she told them over a chorus of barks. 'We'll keep them for as long as it takes.'

'How could anyone choose between them?' Mandy wondered, as she passed cage after cage. German shepherds, terriers, greyhounds, lurchers – and more varieties of mixed-breed dogs than she could ever have imagined – rushed up to greet the visitors. Most of them were barking and wagging their tails furiously, as if pleading for a chance to show just what wonderful pets they would make.

'I'd like to take them all home – every one,' James said, as an eager mongrel tried to lick his fingers through the wire of the cage. 'I don't know what Blackie would think about it, though!'

'I sometimes think it's the dogs who pick their owners,' Penny said. 'You'll often find a dog will react to one particular person very strongly.' She smiled at the mongrel James was petting. 'This little fellow loves everyone, though,' she added.

'Do you ever get depressed, working here?' Mandy asked. She was finding the sight of so many abandoned dogs, desperate for a home, absolutely heartbreaking.

'Not often,' Penny replied. 'This is a very happy place, most of the time! Seeing an animal go off to a new home where you know he'll be loved makes all the difficult times worthwhile. But I do get angry at the state some of the poor things are in when they come to us. And it's sad to see some of our old-timers still here, month after month. Like Spike, for instance.'

She pointed to a large grey dog, curled up in

his basket. He opened one eye as they came up to the cage and lifted his head to watch them, but made no attempt to get up. 'Spike is the sweetest, gentlest creature you could imagine,' Penny explained. 'But as soon as people find out how old he is, they don't want to know.'

'I can't bear that kind of attitude,' Miss Davy said, and Mandy was surprised by the depth of feeling in her voice. 'It's the same with people. Once you've passed a certain age, it's as though you're not good for anything any more. But look at that lovely dog – he's got so much to offer.'

Spike raised his ears and looked at her. Then, slowly, he began to struggle stiffly to his feet.

'Now that's a surprise,' Penny said quietly. 'He doesn't usually bother to get up. It's as though he's given up hope of anyone taking an interest in him.'

Spike climbed out of the basket and padded towards them.

'Has he got some greyhound in him?' James asked. 'Look at those long legs! I bet he can run fast.'

Penny was too busy watching Spike to answer. He'd walked up to the cage door and was sitting there, staring intently at Eileen Davy and slowly wagging the very tip of his tail. Then he barked – just once – and turned to look at Penny. 'Well, how about that?' she said in astonishment.

'Could he come out of the cage for a second?' Mandy asked. 'It would be nice for Spike to have a fuss made of him for once.' An idea was taking shape in her head. Hadn't Penny said the dogs sometimes chose their owners? From what she could see, it certainly looked as though Spike had

chosen Miss Davy. Perhaps it would only take a little encouragement for her to fall for him, too.

'OK,' Penny said, already opening the cage door. 'I'm sure he'd love a bit of attention.'

Spike made a beeline straight for Miss Davy as soon as he was out of the cage. He pushed his head against her smart navy skirt, shedding a couple of pale hairs. Then he sat in front of her and solemnly offered a paw to shake.

'Oh, he's gorgeous, isn't he?' Mandy said. 'He's really taken to you, Miss Davy.'

'He definitely has,' Penny said. 'I've never seen him behave like this before!'

Eileen Davy held Spike's paw and gazed into his appealing eyes. 'I can guess exactly what's going through your mind, Mandy,' she said, in a voice that was rather softer than usual. 'But it's no use, I'm afraid. You can't just adopt a dog on a whim. It's a big commitment, and not one I'm ready to make just now.'

'Oh, Spike would be so happy—' Mandy began, but her father quietly interrupted her by laying his hands firmly on her shoulders.

'Mandy, Miss Davy is right,' he told her firmly. 'You can't force someone into a decision like this.

Not to mention all the practical difficulties! We're on holiday, remember, and we only came here to hand Bruno over. Now I think it's time for us to go.'

Mandy could hardly bear to watch as Penny led Spike back into his cage. She could feel his eyes burning into her back as they turned away, and hear his deep, urgent bark follow them out of the kennel block. *Don't leave me here!* he seemed to be calling. *Just give me a chance!*

They were all quiet on the journey back to The Crow's-Nest. Miss Davy stared out of the train window, lost in thought. Adam Hope fell asleep, and James read his guidebook. Mandy closed her eyes and let images from the dogs' home whirl around inside her head. She tried to think positively. Bruno would be well looked after there, she knew that, and if his owner didn't claim him, Penny would make sure he went to a good home. By the time the train had pulled into Greenwich station, she had convinced herself that Spike would also find a loving family soon. It was too painful to imagine him left at the centre for much longer.

They found Casey sitting in the back garden of The Crow's-Nest. 'You'll never guess what's happened!' Mandy told her. 'We've got the most amazing news!'

Casey laid down the book she'd been reading and squinted up at them from under her baseball cap. 'We've all been invited to tea at Buckingham Palace?' she said. 'The Millennium Dome has blown down in the wind? They've caught a shark in the Thames?'

'We found the puppy!' James announced triumphantly, sitting next to her on the bench. 'We were having a picnic in the park, and there he was!'

'That's great!' Casey exclaimed. 'But it's not so great that I wasn't there! Why didn't you come back and get me?'

'There just wasn't time for that,' Mandy smiled. 'We managed to catch him, and then we took him straight to the dogs' home. They're going to see if anyone claims him, and if not they'll find him a new home. We've given him a name, too – Bruno.'

'Oh, I wish I could take him back to the States!' Casey sighed. 'I feel like Bruno belongs to us, don't you? What was he like? Was he just as cute close-up?'

'He was adorable,' Mandy said. 'Wasn't he, James? It was so hard to part with him.' She fell silent, remembering how she'd felt as they walked away from the dogs' home. There had been two dogs she couldn't bear to leave behind, not just one.

'So what's been happening here?' James asked Casey. 'What have you done today?'

'Not much,' she replied with a huge yawn. 'Certainly nothing as exciting as that. We hung around here in the morning, and then we went shopping in the market this afternoon.'

'That's what Mum and Gran went to do, with Mrs McFarlane,' Mandy said, looking at her watch. 'Are they still not back?'

'Nope, nobody's here except for us and Mac,' Casey replied. 'He's in the kitchen, I think. But listen, I haven't told you the good news. Dad has passed me fit, so I can come to the Millennium Dome with you tomorrow.'

'That's great!' James said. 'I can't wait to see it.' Then a thoughtful look came over his face. 'Do you realise, Mandy,' he went on, 'we've only got two full days left in London? The time's going so quickly!'

'I know,' Mandy said. 'But then, on the other hand, I feel as if we've been here for ever.' She looked round the sunny garden. Patch, the little tortoiseshell cat, was stalking through some tall grasses in the border like a miniature tiger. And there, in the shade of an overhanging lilac tree, stood Sinbad's cage.

'Oh, Sinbad's here!' she said, going up to say hello. 'He's lost his voice all of a sudden.'

'You'll get a shock when you see him,' Casey warned, getting up to follow Mandy over.

Sinbad was sitting on the perch with his back towards them, but he turned around and whistled as they approached. 'Oh no!' Mandy gasped, horrified. 'Sinbad, what's happened to you?'

There were hardly any grey feathers left on his breast, and he'd even plucked away some of the down beneath so that bare skin showed through. He was a pathetic sight to behold – a bedraggled, scrappy-looking creature. 'Hello, Sinbad,' he squawked, as if he were trying to pretend nothing was wrong. Then he turned away again, as though too embarrassed to meet Mandy's eye.

'Mac found him like that in the dining-room this afternoon,' Casey said. 'He's really worried.'

James had come over to join them. 'Why on earth should Sinbad want to do that to himself?' he asked. 'It looks really sore!'

Mandy tried to remember what her mother had said. 'Apparently it's because he's under some kind of stress,' she said, thinking hard. 'But we've got no idea what's causing it.'

'You don't think Patch could be frightening him?' James asked. 'Cats do hunt birds, don't they? Perhaps he thinks she's after him.'

Casey shook her head. 'No, Mac told me they get on really well,' she said. 'Sinbad was here first, and he soon showed Patch who was boss. They're the best of friends now.'

Mandy remembered the first time they'd met Sinbad. It seemed ridiculous now to think that they'd been so frightened. Surely it couldn't just have been one parrot all by itself that had made them feel like that. What else was there? 'Come on!' she said suddenly. 'I think we need to go to the dining-room.'

'Why?' Casey asked as Mandy hurried them inside. 'What's there that we have to see in such a rush?'

'I'm not sure yet,' Mandy replied, throwing open

the door. 'But I think we need to get inside Sinbad's skin. There's something in this room that's making him uncomfortable, I'm sure of it. We felt it too, James, the first time we met him. We were scared, and it wasn't just because he was squawking at us.'

The three of them stared around the room. Then they all looked back at each other and said at exactly the same time, 'Daisy May!'

'She's lovely, isn't she?' Mac said, passing by on his way out of the kitchen with a tray of tea. 'I got her in the antiques market a couple of months ago.'

'No, you don't understand!' Mandy said, stumbling in her eagerness to get the words out. 'That's why Sinbad is so unhappy. He's on his own with her for most of the day, and he doesn't like it.'

Mac stared at her for a few seconds without speaking. 'Do you think so?' he said eventually. 'Come on, she's only a carving. I think she's beautiful.'

'She *is* beautiful,' Mandy replied eagerly, pulling him into the dining-room to face the figurehead. 'But, look – don't you think she's a bit threatening, too? Sinbad doesn't know she's not real. I think he's terrified of her.'

'We're certain that's it!' Casey added, speaking for all three of them.

'I suppose he does spend most of his time in here,' Mac said, putting the tray down on a side table and scratching his beard while he looked at Daisy May. He sighed. 'It was a big job getting her up on that wall. But if it'll help Sinbad, she'll just have to come down again.'

'But Sinbad's cage is on wheels,' James said. 'Why don't you put him somewhere else for the time being and see what happens?'

'Like the hall,' Mandy suggested, remembering the first time they'd seen Patch hiding behind the globe. 'There's so much to look at there, and people are coming and going all day. He'd get loads of attention!'

'Of course!' Mac said. 'I've just got so used to Sinbad being in this room that I've never considered moving him. But maybe he is a bit lonely here. And now I come to think of it, he did take a turn for the worse around the time that Daisy May arrived. I wonder if you could be right . . .'

'Oh, I hope we are,' Mandy said, thinking of the poor moth-eaten parrot out in the garden. 'We can't let Sinbad carry on hurting himself!'

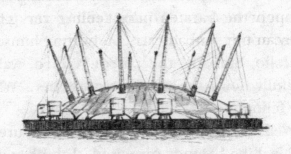

Eight

Mandy woke up the next morning to sunlight streaming in through her curtains, and a strange sound floating up from downstairs. She quickly pulled some clothes on, trying not to disturb her gran who was still asleep, and crept out of the room.

'The sun has got his hat on,' Sinbad was squawking merrily, 'hip, hip, hip hooray! The sun has got his hat on and he's coming out today.' Mac had moved away a coatstand and put the parrot's cage in a corner of the hall, near a side window that looked out on to the street.

'Hello there, Sinbad,' she said, smiling at him through the bars. 'You're feeling very chirpy today, aren't you?'

'Hello, Sinbad!' the parrot replied, walking carefully down the perch to greet her. 'What a fine fellow!'

'Well, maybe not quite yet, but I'm sure you soon will be,' Mandy promised. 'I think you like it better here, don't you?'

'Oh, he's a different bird already,' Mac said, coming into the hall with a tea towel over his shoulder. 'This is the perfect place for him! It's not too draughty, and he can watch what's going on outside too. He's already made friends with the postman.'

'Mac! Mac!' Sinbad ordered as soon as he caught sight of his owner. 'Come here, boy.'

'That means he wants a tickle,' Mac told Mandy. 'I'm busy,' he called back to the parrot, but Sinbad just squawked his name again – even louder this time.

'OK, you old rascal,' Mac replied, putting down the towel and going over to open the cage door. Gently, he reached in to scratch the tiny feathers that overlapped each other like silvery chain mail on the top of Sinbad's head. 'I'm just kicking myself for not having thought of it before,' he went on. 'Sinbad's back to his old self, even if he is going to look a mess for a while longer. Thanks for solving the mystery, Mandy.'

'Oh, I'm just glad he seems to be better,' she said. 'Let's hope those feathers don't take too long to grow back.'

'You can get a cardboard collar from the vet's,' Emily Hope advised Mac, overhearing their conversation as she came down the stairs. 'Just to make sure he gets out of the habit of pecking himself.'

'I will,' Mac said, walking back towards the kitchen. 'Just as soon as I've finished the breakfasts. I thought we'd have waffles this morning, to celebrate.'

'We're going to miss Mac's cooking,' Mrs Hope said, putting an arm round Mandy's shoulders. 'But just look at this parrot! He certainly seems to like it here in the hall.'

Sinbad walked back down the perch and then suddenly picked his way up a rope at the side of the cage to swing upside down from the top, hooking his claws through the bars. 'Hello,

Sinbad,' he squawked again, looking cheekily back and making them both laugh.

'So, Mandy, there's nothing left for you to worry about,' her mother said, giving her a squeeze. 'Sinbad's going to get better and you found your runaway pup. Now you can really enjoy the last couple of days here.'

'I will!' Mandy replied, turning away from the cage. 'I wish we could have seen Bruno back together with his owner, but at least we know he's safe.'

'And we're going to visit the Dome today,' her mother reminded her. 'I can't wait to see what it's like inside!'

A couple of hours later, full of waffles and maple syrup, everyone wandered down the street to catch a bus that would take them the short distance to the Dome.

'Are Walter and Ernie coming?' Mandy asked her grandmother as they waited at the bus stop. 'We've hardly seen them this holiday.'

'Yes, we're going to meet them outside the Dome at ten, along with Mrs McFarlane,' her gran replied. 'I rang the pub last night to arrange it.'

She laughed. 'I think they've had enough of city life. Ernie said he would never have guessed how noisy London was.'

'D'you know, I'm looking forward to going back too,' Casey confided to Mandy and James. 'We've had a great time here, and I'm so glad I've met you both, but there's no place like home, is there?'

'No, there isn't,' Mandy agreed, thinking rather wistfully about Animal Ark. She looked around the bustling street, thronging with traffic and overlooked by terraced houses and blocks of flats. How different her life would have been if she'd been adopted by a family who lived in the city! It made her head spin just thinking about it.

Then a huddled figure sitting in a doorway near the bus stop caught her eye. 'Buy a magazine and help the homeless?' the man asked, waving a copy in her direction.

'Sure,' Mandy said, fumbling for her purse. She still had most of her spending money left over and, besides, they'd just been talking about how much they were all looking forward to going home. Here was someone who didn't have a home at all and Mandy wanted to help.

'Thanks, love,' said the man, handing over the

magazine. 'Have a nice day! Where are you off to?'

'We're going to the Millennium Dome,' Mandy said. 'Oh, can I say hello to your dog?' A bright-looking little terrier was sleeping on a blanket at the man's feet.

'Course you can,' he replied, tucking Mandy's pound coin away in his pocket. 'She won't bite. Her name's Lucy, if you want to introduce yourself. And I'm Joe.'

'Hello, Lucy,' Mandy said solemnly, patting the dog's head. 'My name's Mandy. It's nice to meet you.'

James and Casey came over to join them, and they each bought a magazine too. Lucy wagged her stumpy tail ten to the dozen, delighted with all the attention she was getting.

'Oh, she's gorgeous!' Casey said to Joe. 'If she's not careful, she'll wag that tail right off!'

'How long have you had her?' Mandy asked.

'I found her in a dustbin last year,' Joe said, stroking his dog with a grimy hand. 'Someone had dumped her, along with the rubbish. But I took her to the animal hospital and she's fine now. We're company for each other, Lucy and me.

I wouldn't be without her for the world.'

'It can't be easy to look after her sometimes,' James said shyly. 'I mean, if she's ill or anything.'

'We get by,' Joe said. 'She's had all her jabs and I take her back to the animal hospital if she gets any problems. It's easier in the summer but we make it through the winter as best we can. She's a good little hot-water bottle, that's for sure!' He looked over to the bus stop. 'Oh, it looks like that's your bus. Better not miss it!'

Mandy's parents were calling them over. 'Coming!' Mandy shouted back. She looked at the money in her purse. Suddenly the idea of spending it on tacky plastic souvenirs didn't seem such a good one. 'Here,' she said, giving Joe a five-pound note. 'Can you put this towards a coat for Lucy? She might be glad of one when it gets colder.'

'Well, thanks very much,' said Joe, delighted. His smile grew even broader when James and Casey added their own money to the collection. 'She'll have the warmest coat in London this winter,' he promised, holding Lucy up and waving goodbye as they got on the bus. 'Come and visit again and you'll see!'

They waved back out of the window as the bus pulled away. 'It's great to come across someone who really cares about their dog,' James commented, as Joe and Lucy grew smaller in the distance. 'Especially after all those poor strays we saw yesterday.'

'I was just thinking exactly the same,' Mandy agreed. 'Lucy might not have regular meals or a warm bed, but I'd say she was a lot better off than Spike. She's got someone who loves her, and that's more important than anything.'

'Look, there's the Dome!' Mandy's dad said as

the white mushroom shape, familiar from so many photographs, came into view. But Mandy was still thinking about Spike, though. She hoped he and Bruno would soon have owners to love them as much as Joe obviously loved Lucy. But, somehow, she wasn't convinced.

Nine

'Now what are we going to do on our last day in London?' Adam Hope asked, looking round the breakfast table the following morning.

'It's a pity the weather's not a bit better,' said Mandy's gran, gazing out at the cloudy sky. 'Mrs Ponsonby's got her famous garden party this afternoon. I hope her new hat doesn't get wet, or we'll never hear the end of it!'

'Why don't we take a bus trip round London?' James suggested. 'I noticed special sightseeing buses at the station. You can get on and off them wherever you like, and they take you to all the famous places.' Suddenly, realising that everyone's eyes were on him, he stopped and looked rather embarrassed. 'But I don't mind if no one else wants to,' he said. 'It's just an idea.'

'Well, I think it's a very good one,' Emily Hope said, draining her cup of tea. 'We had such a busy time yesterday. Watching the world go by from a seat on the bus is just what I feel like doing!'

'Me too,' Mandy said. 'Why don't we all go? I'm sure the Baxters would like to come, and we have to spend our last day with Casey. We could get Walter and Ernie along, too, and Miss Davy and Mrs McFarlane. Then we could all go out for a meal this evening. What do you say, Gran?'

'I'd say you two had better plan next year's trip!' laughed her grandmother. 'It all sounds perfect, dear. I'll give Walter and Ernie a ring – I'm sure they'd love to come.'

It didn't seem long before everyone was sitting upstairs on the open top deck of a sightseeing bus. The sun was just breaking through the clouds as they pulled away to start the tour.

'Would you just look at that traffic!' Ernie said, looking down at the road as they approached

Trafalgar Square. 'Those cars are packed solid!'

'Where are we now?' Casey asked James. 'I didn't hear what the guide said. What's that big pillar coming up?'

'That's Nelson's Column,' James replied. 'This is one of the places I thought we could stop off at for a while. I really want to take some photos of those big stone lions at the bottom.'

'Sounds good to me,' Mandy said, getting up from her seat as the bus drew to a halt. 'Who's coming?'

It turned out that everyone wanted to see the lions at the foot of Nelson's Column and have a wander round Trafalgar Square. There were flocks of pigeons everywhere and even a couple of seagulls, wheeling round the fountains. After James had taken a few shots, he decided to get everyone together for a group picture. 'Mr Pickard and Mr Bell, could you stand at the back,' he called. 'Then Mandy and Casey in the middle, please, with everyone else sort of gathered around.'

'Do you want my cap on or off?' Walter Pickard called out obligingly.

'Off, I think,' James replied from behind the

camera. But then, instead of taking the photo, he lowered his camera and stood peering at something behind them.

'Oh, come on, James!' Mandy called impatiently. 'We've been standing here for ever. Hurry up and take the picture so I can go and feed the pigeons!'

But James just carried on standing still, holding the camera loosely by his side and staring at the fountain behind them on the other side of the square. 'I don't believe it!' he said, pointing towards it.

Mandy turned to look. She rubbed her eyes and looked again. Surely, it couldn't be? But there, splashing happily around in the fountain, was a mischievous little brown Labrador puppy. 'Bruno!' she gasped in amazement. 'But that's impossible!'

'Now this is someone I have to meet!' Casey said, striding towards the fountain. 'After all, I missed out last time.'

'Careful, Casey!' Mandy warned, rushing along after her. 'He's quite nervous and he could easily run out into the road. There are cars everywhere!'

The puppy was romping through the shallow water, sending up showers of spray and drenching a small group of tourists that had gathered to watch him play. They didn't seem to mind, though. Cameras were clicking and everyone was smiling at the adorable little dog.

'Here, boy!' Casey whistled. 'Come here, Bruno.'

To Mandy's surprise, the puppy splashed obediently towards her, pink tongue hanging out of one side of his mouth as he bounded over.

'Well, you're not nervous with me, are you?' Casey said, as she patted him. 'You are *so* cute! I don't even mind the fact you're making me wet through.'

Mandy stared at the Labrador pup, still hardly able to take in what she was seeing. There were a few muddy patches on his damp coat, but he seemed to be in good spirits and otherwise unhurt.

'You should keep your dog on a lead,' an elderly woman said severely to Mandy, turning back to look disapprovingly at Casey over the top of her glasses. 'He could cause a nasty accident.'

'He's not exactly our dog,' Mandy began, unable to take her eyes off the puppy. Casey was holding him securely while he shook himself, sending silver droplets of water flying through the air. By now, Mandy's parents and the Baxters had come over, followed by Miss Davy and the others.

'Pass me your tie, please, Dad,' Casey asked her father. 'We need an emergency lead here.'

'What on earth is this little fellow doing here?' Mr Hope exclaimed. 'The last time we saw him, he was safely in his cage at the dogs' home!' He gave the puppy a quick look over. 'Well, his ear seems fine now,' he said. 'That's something, I suppose.'

'We'll have to tell the dogs' home we've found him again,' Mandy said, crouching down to have a good look at Bruno as he sat by Casey's feet, the tip of his tail wagging furiously. 'He must have escaped somehow.'

'But how has he found his way here?' James wondered. 'Think of all the traffic he's had to get through.'

'Well, however he managed it, I think we need to take him back to the home right away, don't you?' Miss Davy said. 'They must be very worried about him going missing. Come on, this time it's my turn to pay for the taxi.' And she started walking towards the road to look for one.

'What about our sightseeing trip?' Ernie said. 'There's another bus stopped over there – we could have caught it.'

'Why don't the rest of you go on without us?' Adam Hope replied. 'Let's arrange to meet up again at that café in St James's Park for lunch. About one o'clock?'

'Well, if you're sure you don't mind taking care of our daughter,' said Dr Baxter. 'And Casey, that's my favourite tie. I want it back again!'

Miss Davy soon managed to hail a taxi, and everyone went over towards it. The little pup bounded along at Casey's side, quite happy to come along with them. Miss Davy held open the door and he hopped in and sat on the back seat as though he'd been riding in taxis all his life.

The taxi driver muttered something grumpily. 'You'll have to squash up,' he said over his shoulder in a louder voice. 'Five passengers is the most I'm allowed to take, and that's not counting any dogs. And I hope he's not making a mess of my upholstery.'

'Come on, Bruno,' Mandy said, scooping him on to her lap. 'You'd better sit here with me.' She laid her cheek against his smooth brown head and added, 'No more running off on your own now – OK?'

'There's something really strange about this,' Mandy said, as they waited for Penny to meet them in the reception area at the dogs' home. She took another long look at the puppy, who was busy winding Dr Baxter's best tie into knots as he explored an interesting corner behind the chair.

'You're telling me!' James replied. 'I still can't believe Bruno managed to get all the way from here to Trafalgar Square. It's on the other side of the river!'

'And without getting run over or caught,' said Mandy's father. 'That really is incredible. Maybe someone befriended him, but then why didn't they take him into a police station?'

'There's something else, though,' Mandy went on. 'He seems so different now – much more confident and bouncy. Look how easy it was to catch him. He got really spooked when we went after him on Monday.' She clicked her fingers and the pup immediately came running up to sniff them. 'See what I mean?' she said.

'It's because I'm here, of course,' Casey joked, giving the pup a cuddle. 'I've got a way with dogs. If I'd been around last time, you wouldn't have had any problems.'

Before Mandy could think of a witty reply, Penny appeared. 'Well, hello again,' she said. 'Have you come to visit Bruno? He's still feeling pretty miserable, I'm afraid.'

'What do you mean?' James replied. He pointed towards the puppy, who had started to run in circles around Casey's feet. 'Look! Bruno's here with us.'

Penny gave a start as soon as she caught sight of the little dog. 'But that's impossible!' she exclaimed. 'I don't believe it!'

'Neither could we,' Mandy said. 'We found him splashing around in the fountain in Trafalgar Square just now. Didn't you know he'd gone missing?'

'He isn't missing, though!' Penny said. 'I've just walked past Bruno, asleep in his cage in the holding block. You were right, by the way – he did have a grass seed in his ear. We got it out just in time.' She gave the puppy a pat, looking intently at him. 'Well,' she said, smiling up at their astonished faces, 'this little fellow's just as gorgeous, but he's not our Bruno.'

They all stared at her for a moment, unable to take in this amazing piece of news.

'So that's why you thought there was something different about him, Mandy,' said Adam Hope. 'He's another dog altogether!'

'Which means there are two lost puppies,' Mandy said slowly. 'And we've found both of them.'

The pup began to wind his makeshift lead around Casey's legs, worrying away at it with sharp white teeth. 'Hold on there, fella,' she said. 'My dad's going to kill me if you eat his tie.'

'I think you'd better come with me and we'll check him in,' Penny said, bending down to give the puppy a quick examination. 'Then we can give him a proper collar and his own number. It'll be hard to tell him and Bruno apart.'

'They must be from the same litter, don't you think?' Mandy said, crouching down beside her. 'Same age, same colouring. And Trafalgar Square isn't that far from St James's Park – where we picked up Bruno.'

'So no one's reported losing any Labrador puppies yet?' Miss Davy asked.

'No, they haven't,' Penny replied, giving the puppy a final stroke and straightening up. 'I really can't understand it. These two have obviously come from a good home, and they're so appealing. I'd have thought they'd have been claimed straight away, but no one's contacted the police or the RSPCA, or any of the local vets. It's very strange.'

It certainly is, Mandy thought. *If those two puppies*

belonged to me, I wouldn't let them out of my sight!

'I'll just check this pup in and then we can take him to see Bruno,' Penny went on. 'Come with me and we'll get the forms filled out. I'm sure you remember the process from last time!'

'Perhaps we should call him Nelson for the time being,' James suggested as they followed Penny into the main part of the home. 'After all, we were standing by Nelson's Column when we saw him. Nelson and Bruno – what do you think?'

'I think that sounds great,' Mandy replied, looking at the bouncy little pup as he scampered along beside them, nose to the ground in search of interesting smells. 'Nelson really suits him somehow.'

'Nelson it is, then,' Casey said, giving James a pat on the back.

'Who knows, maybe their owner will turn up soon and we'll find out what their real names are,' Penny added over her shoulder.

'Oh, I hope so,' Mandy sighed. She couldn't shake off the feeling that someone, somewhere, must be desperate to find both Nelson and his brother.

* * *

'Well, those two are certainly happy to see each other!' Casey commented as they watched the two puppies playing together. As soon as Bruno had caught sight of Nelson, he'd rushed up to the cage door and thrown himself against it, whining and barking excitedly. Now the two of them were tearing round the kennel, wrestling each other to the ground with lots of playful nips and growls. James took photo after photo until he ran out of Polaroid film.

'Bruno'll be so much happier to have some company,' Mandy said. 'Leaving him behind doesn't feel as bad now Nelson's with him.'

'I promise I'll give you a ring and tell you what happens to them,' Penny said as she bolted the cage door. 'When are you going home?'

'Tomorrow morning,' Mandy said. 'And Casey and her parents are leaving the day after that.' She took one long last look at the two puppies, now curled up together on the blanket. 'Oh, I hope they'll be OK!'

'We'll look after them, don't you worry,' Penny reassured her as they began to walk away.

'Actually, there is just one more thing,' Miss Davy said, and something about the tone of her voice made everyone stop and look at her. 'I don't want to hold you all up,' she went on, taking a deep breath, 'but I would like to see Spike again before we go.'

'Oh, Miss Davy!' Mandy breathed, hardly daring to hope. 'You don't mean—'

'Yes, I do,' Eileen Davy said firmly. She turned to Penny. 'I've been thinking this over very carefully, and I *would* like to offer him a home. If you think mine would be suitable, that is.'

Before Penny could say anything in reply, Mandy had thrown her arms round Miss Davy and given her a big hug. 'Oh, that's wonderful!' she cried. 'He'll be so happy with you, I know he will! We'll help you walk him, and Mum and Dad can look after him in the surgery if he needs anything—'

'Steady on, Mandy!' Miss Davy said, though her eyes were shining and she didn't look at all cross. 'I'm sure there are a lot of questions Penny needs to ask. I haven't been approved yet! But I haven't been able to get that dear old dog out of my mind, and coming back here for the second time seems like fate. I think I'm meant to have him.'

Penny was smiling too. 'You're right, there are a lot of things we need to discuss,' she said. 'But

I'm delighted you feel this way, and Spike will be too. I'm sure we can work it all out!'

'That's marvellous news, Eileen,' Mr Hope said, and soon everyone was patting Miss Davy on the back and shaking her hand.

'Even if everything goes smoothly, you won't be able to take him away just yet, I'm afraid,' Penny warned. 'But we can certainly start the ball rolling now. Come back to my room for a moment and we'll get going on the forms.'

'Why don't we wait for you in the café here?' Mandy's dad suggested. 'I could do with a cup of tea after all this excitement!'

They were just finishing their drinks by the time Miss Davy came back. She looked as neat and composed as usual but, underneath, Mandy could tell she was feeling very emotional. 'Well, someone from the home is going to visit me next week,' she informed them. 'If all goes well, I could have Spike with me in Welford by the end of the month. There are my hens to consider, of course, but Penny tells me he's much too good to chase them. He really is the most delightful dog!'

'And we'd never have met him if it wasn't for

the puppies,' Mandy said. 'Oh, Miss Davy, you are lucky!' She turned to her father, determined to try one question out on him, although she already had a very good idea what the answer would be.

'Dad,' she began, 'if the puppies' owner doesn't turn up, do you think there's any way . . .'

'No, Mandy, I'm sorry,' her father replied firmly. 'Hold it right there. They're beautiful dogs, but there's no way we can take them on. I know it seems hard, but we just can't—'

'Oh, thank goodness I caught you before you left!' Penny came bursting through the swing doors and rushed up to their table. She sank down on a chair next to them to catch her breath. 'I've just taken a call from a woman who's lost her puppies,' she went on. 'They're Labradors – chocolate-coloured ones. I think we've found Nelson and Bruno's owner! She's on her way over here now, and she wants to talk to you. Can you wait?'

Ten

'Oh, please can we stay here a little longer?' Mandy begged her father. 'I couldn't bear not to know whether Nelson and Bruno really have been claimed!'

'I should think so,' Adam Hope replied. 'We've come this far, so we may as well find out how the story ends.' He looked at his watch and added, 'We might be a bit late meeting the others for lunch, but I'm sure they won't mind waiting.'

'Don't worry,' said Miss Davy, getting to her feet. 'I'll go back to the park and let them know you've been delayed. To be honest, I want to share my good news with everyone. You can tell me later what happens with the puppies.'

'Their owner – if she really is their owner – doesn't live far away,' Penny said, after Miss Davy had left. 'It won't take her very long to get here. Apparently she's some famous writer, though I hadn't heard of her. Jane, our switchboard operator, recognised the name.' She looked down at the notepad she was holding. 'Where is it now? Yes, here we are: Laura Dawson.'

'*What?*' James and Mandy exclaimed together. 'Laura Dawson? Not *the* Laura Dawson?'

'Looks like it,' Penny said, grinning at their startled faces. 'Jane says her son's a big fan. He's got all the books she's ever written.'

'You know Laura Dawson!' Mandy said excitedly, turning to Casey. 'She's the author of all those fantastic animal stories – the *Sweetwater Sanctuary* series and the *Running Wild* books, and loads of others. You're reading one of hers at the moment. I saw you, in the garden the other day.'

'Of course!' Casey said. 'So that's why her name sounded familiar. Wow! It's such a great story, and I'm going to meet the person who wrote it! Now I really do have something to tell everyone back home.'

Mandy stared into the distance. 'To think, we might actually have rescued Laura Dawson's puppies,' she said in a faraway voice. 'I can't believe it.'

'Well, it sounds like she could do with some advice on looking after them,' said Emily Hope. 'Brilliant writer or not.'

'I agree,' Penny said. 'There are a few things we need to ask Laura Dawson when she arrives. If Nelson and Bruno do belong to her, she's lucky to be getting them back in one piece.'

'There has to be some explanation,' Mandy said stubbornly. Laura Dawson was her favourite author. She wrote so beautifully about animals – surely she would know how to take care of her own?

Fifteen minutes later, a slim, anxious-looking woman with a large bag slung over one shoulder came rushing into the dogs' home. The swing doors banged noisily behind her. James, Casey, Mr Hope and Mandy had moved over from the café to wait for Laura Dawson in the reception area, and Mandy realised immediately that the famous writer had just arrived. She'd once seen her photograph on a poster in a bookshop.

'My name is Laura Dawson,' the woman said, hurrying up to the reception desk. 'I think you may have my puppies.'

Mandy felt James nudge her side urgently. 'There she is!' he hissed. 'Go on, say something!'

'Take a seat and someone will be with you shortly,' the receptionist answered calmly, picking up her phone.

Laura Dawson walked towards them. Mandy had a quick impression of piercing blue eyes, fair skin and dark wavy hair gathered back into a loose plait. 'Um, Ms Dawson,' she began, standing up. 'We, er, found your puppies and brought them here. If they are yours, that is. I'm Mandy Hope, and these are my friends James and Casey, and my father—'

'Oh, Mandy, I'm so glad to meet you!' Laura Dawson said. She smiled hello at all of them and then took Mandy's hand in her own for a moment. 'I don't know how to thank you enough, really I don't. And please, do call me Laura. I've been out of my mind with worry—'

'Why didn't you report them missing?' Mandy blurted out. 'We can't understand why no one's come for them till now.'

'Mandy!' James exclaimed, looking horrified that she should dare to say such a thing – to Laura Dawson, of all people.

'I'm sorry,' Mandy went on. 'It's just that anything could have happened to the puppies, running round London on their own. It's a miracle they weren't run over.'

'But I only found out they were lost an hour ago!' Laura Dawson exclaimed, rubbing a hand anxiously across her forehead. 'I came as soon as I could.'

Mandy stared at her uncertainly. How could that possibly be true? They'd first seen Bruno at Buckingham Palace on Saturday – five days ago.

Penny came into the reception area. 'You must be Ms Dawson,' she said, sounding very formal and just a little bit disapproving. 'Would you like to come with me now and I'll take you to the puppies?'

'Yes, of course!' Laura said, jumping to her feet. 'Oh, I do hope they're mine – they've just got to be! You must let me explain—'

'Why don't we talk on the way over?' Penny said, holding the door open. 'I'm sure you'd like to see the dogs as soon as possible.'

'Can everybody else come along?' Laura asked. 'I've got so many questions to ask.'

'I'll stay and wait for you here,' Adam Hope volunteered. 'It might be better not to have too many people crowding around.'

Penny led the way down the corridor and Mandy, James and Casey followed on behind with Laura Dawson.

'How come you've only just discovered the puppies had strayed?' Mandy asked her as they walked off. Laura was so warm and friendly, she didn't feel intimidated by her at all.

'Because I've been away on a publicity tour and didn't get back 'til this morning,' Ms Dawson replied, hoisting up her enormous bag as it slid down one shoulder. 'I've been giving interviews about my new series and signing copies – all that commotion.'

'*Every Living Thing*, you mean?' James asked, his eyes shining excitedly behind his glasses. 'I've got the first book at home. It's brilliant!'

'I'm glad you like it,' Laura Dawson replied, with a quick smile. 'Well, I went away on Saturday and left the dogs at home with my housekeeper. Apparently, she'd given them a bath and taken their collars off.' She patted her bag and added, 'I've brought them with me, and their leads too. Oh, I do so hope these really are my puppies!' She paused and bit her lip before carrying on. 'Anyway, they were running around the garden to dry off in the sun, and the side gate had been left open. That must have been how they escaped.'

'And your housekeeper didn't let you know?' Casey asked. 'Or report it to the police?'

'She thought she could find them on her own before I got back, and then I'd never need to know,' Laura replied. 'She kept ringing the police to see if anyone had brought them in, but wouldn't leave her details in case I got to hear of it. And she didn't think to contact the dogs' home, I'm afraid.'

'Well, here we are,' Penny said as she opened the door to the holding block. 'Let's hope the story has a happy ending.' Suddenly, the air exploded into a frenzy of barks and whines as the dogs inside greeted their visitors.

'We've called them Nelson and Bruno,' Penny went on, walking towards the puppies' cage, 'though you may be able to tell us what their real names are.'

Laura Dawson followed Penny. Mandy realised

she could hardly bear to look at the cage, in case she'd discover the puppies inside belonged to someone else. Nelson had rushed up to the wire and was standing there, wagging his tail, while Bruno hung back behind him. As soon as they saw Laura, they burst into high-pitched, excited barks, throwing themselves against the door in their eagerness to get at her.

'Oh, yes!' she exclaimed, crouching down to their level. 'These are mine – George and Henry! Thank goodness they're safe!' Penny opened the cage door and the two little dogs rushed out into Laura's waiting arms, nearly knocking her over in their excitement. 'Stop it! Enough!' she laughed, as they tried to lick every inch of her face.

'That's wonderful!' Mandy said, swapping delighted smiles with James and Casey as they watched the happy reunion. There could be no doubt at all that these were Laura Dawson's puppies, and that they were as overjoyed to see her as she was to find them.

'So where's Princess?' Laura asked, looking up at Penny as the two dogs tumbled over each other in her lap. 'Is this cage too small for three? Are you keeping her somewhere else?'

'I'm sorry?' Penny said blankly. 'Who's Princess? These are the only Labrador puppies we have.'

Mandy felt a cold chill sink into her stomach. She saw the joy in Laura's face slowly fade as she stammered, 'But I have three dogs – George, Henry and Princess. Didn't you find them all together?'

'No, I'm afraid we didn't,' Mandy replied, kneeling down beside Laura and trying to calm the puppies while she explained. 'We saw one of the pups at Buckingham Palace first, on Saturday, and then we spotted one in Victoria Street the next day. But we only managed to catch this fellow on Monday, in St James's Park. He's the one we called Bruno.' And she picked out the more timid of the two pups.

'That's Henry,' Laura said, hugging him to her. 'So he was all on his own?'

'Yes! We didn't find his brother until this morning, in Trafalgar Square,' Mandy said. 'At first, we thought he must have been Bruno – I mean, Henry – who'd escaped from the dogs' home. We didn't realise there were two puppies.'

'And we had no idea there were three!' James put in. 'Where on earth could Princess be?'

'That's what we'll have to work out,' Mandy said determinedly. 'We've found George and Henry – now we have to find their sister!'

'The thing is, we don't know which puppy we saw where,' Mandy said, looking at the circle of intent faces round the table. The two Labrador pups had been checked out of the dogs' home and now everyone was back in the café, trying to decide what to do next. Laura Dawson was sipping a cup of tea while Henry sat as close to her as he possibly could, resting his head on her lap. George lay on his back under the table, looking blissfully happy as James scratched his tummy.

'The puppies are so alike!' Mandy went on. 'It could have been Princess we saw at Buckingham Palace or in Victoria Street, or maybe we haven't seen her at all. We just don't know!'

'Let's go through everything once again,' Casey suggested. She turned to Laura. 'The pups all escaped from your house on Saturday morning. And that's in Victoria Square, right? Just behind the Palace?'

'That's right,' Laura answered distractedly. 'And

now it's Wednesday! It's awful to think of them being lost for all this time.'

'Well, at least these two turned up safe and sound in the end,' Mr Hope said encouragingly. 'Let's hope Princess will too.'

'Perhaps we should try and work out whether we might have seen her anywhere,' Mandy said. 'Is there anything unusual about her? Any distinguishing marks?'

Laura shook her head, as if trying to clear it. 'She's a little bit smaller than her brothers,' she said, stroking Henry's ear. 'But they do look very similar, chocolate brown all over.' She thought for another few seconds and then said slowly, 'There is one thing, I suppose. Princess has a real Labrador grin. You know how they seem to smile when they're pleased to see you? Well, she could smile for England.'

'My photos!' James exclaimed, reaching inside his rucksack. 'Of course! Why didn't I think of that before?' He pulled out a sheaf of pictures and started leafing through them. 'There!' he said, pulling out one of the early prints. 'Do you recognise Princess? Could this be her?'

Laura Dawson fumbled in her bag and came

out with a pair of gold-rimmed glasses. She put them on and looked intently at the photo, while Mandy craned over her shoulder to see it too. The little Labrador puppy gazed back out of the photograph at them, head to one side and one ear raised enquiringly. Mandy could just make out the tip of a pink tongue, and the beginnings of a doggy smile.

'That's Princess!' Laura said delightedly. 'No doubt about it – there she is.' She took off her glasses and smiled as she put them back in her bag. 'At Buckingham Palace, of all places!'

'Well, she has the right name for it,' Adam Hope said, tucking into his sandwich. 'But that photo was taken a few days ago. I wonder where she is now?'

'She might still be there,' Mandy suggested. She thought back to when they'd first seen the pup, bounding through the archway below the balcony and on into the grounds beyond. 'After all, Buckingham Palace probably seems like paradise to her. According to James's guidebook there are gardens at the back, with a lake.'

'And these puppies do seem very adventurous,' James added. 'Remember where we found the other two.'

'It's not exactly the easiest place to search though, is it?' Casey said, draining her can of lemonade. 'We can't just go up to the gate and say, "Excuse me, Your Majesty, but we think our dog's in your garden. Can we have a look for her?"'

'No, we can't,' Mandy said, thinking hard. 'But somebody we know is going to Buckingham Palace this afternoon, isn't she?'

'Mrs Ponsonby!' James said, with a broad smile. 'Of course!'

'Look, I don't want to pour cold water on your brilliant idea, Mandy,' said her father, 'but we don't even know what time Mrs Ponsonby's meant to be at Buckingham Palace. By the time we get over there, she may well have gone inside.'

'Then I think we should wait for her to come out,' Mandy said. 'Oh, I know there's only a slim chance of finding Princess there, but it's worth a try, isn't it? And there's no way we could get inside the Palace ourselves.'

'Well, we should be getting back to St James's Park now,' Mr Hope said, looking at his watch again. 'The others must be getting tired of waiting for us.'

'I wish I could give you a lift,' said Laura, standing up and untangling the puppies' leads. They sprang to their feet, looking up at her expectantly as though they were eager to get home. 'I couldn't possibly fit you all in my car, though.' Then, fumbling in her bag, she said rather awkwardly, 'I would like to offer you a reward for all the trouble you've taken. Please, would you accept a token of my gratitude?'

'Oh, no! Please don't,' Mandy said, and saw her father was shaking his head too. 'It's been enough of a reward meeting you – and George and Henry, of course!'

'Well then, at least let me pay for your taxi fares,' Laura said, pressing a note into Mr Hope's hand, despite all his protests. 'I'd better get the puppies home now,' she went on, 'but after I've made sure they're OK, why don't I come back and meet you outside the Palace? There must be something I can do to help.'

'Fine,' Mandy said. 'We'll be there, however long it takes. Princess has got to be inside, I'm sure of it. We just have to find her and get her out. Or rather, Mrs Ponsonby has to – though she doesn't know it yet!'

Eleven

'Just give us a little time. Please, Dad!' Mandy begged, after the taxi had dropped them off on the pavement outside Buckingham Palace. 'I'm sure Mrs Ponsonby will be coming out soon.'

'I'll meet you back here in half an hour,' Adam Hope replied, turning towards St James's Park. 'But no longer. We really can't expect Mum and the others to hang around in the park all day.

'If you three haven't found Mrs Ponsonby by then, you'll have to give up,' he added. 'Don't worry, if the puppy is still somewhere around the

Palace, I'm sure someone will find her sooner or later.'

'So what does this Mrs Ponsonby look like?' Casey asked when Mr Hope had gone, looking at the steady stream of visitors coming out of a side exit. They were all smartly dressed, the men in dark suits and the women in flowery dresses and hats.

'She's quite large, and she'll be wearing a hat with pink and purple ostrich feathers,' Mandy said. She'd heard Mrs Ponsonby describe her garden party outfit a hundred times. 'It should be fairly easy to spot her. And she'll have a little Pekinese dog with her too.'

A few minutes later, there was a shout from Casey. 'There's the hat!' she cried, as the pink and purple feathered creation bobbed towards them through the crowd. 'You can't miss it. There's no sign of a dog, though.'

'Mrs Ponsonby!' Mandy cried, rushing up to her with James and Casey close behind. 'Thank goodness we've found you. Please, we need your help!'

'Is there anything the matter?' James asked, for Mrs Ponsonby was looking decidedly cross. Her face was flushed and she was frowning as she marched along. Casey stared at her in amazement.

'I was not allowed to bring Pandora to the garden party,' Mrs Ponsonby said indignantly. 'I had to take her back to my hotel, and she was most upset about being left behind. By the time I returned to the Palace, I'd lost my place in the queue and all the chocolate cake had gone. And I only caught the merest glimpse of royalty!'

'Oh dear, that's a shame,' Mandy said, trying not to sound too impatient. 'But, please, we really need you to go back—'

'There was no earthly reason why Pandora could not have accompanied me,' Mrs Ponsonby went on. 'The party was held outside, after all. And on top of everything else, there was a puppy running around the Palace gardens! A puppy – just like the one you found in the park! Not wearing a collar, and quite out of control. Nobody could catch it.'

'Yes!' Mandy cried triumphantly. 'The puppy! That's why we need you to help us. Oh please, Mrs Ponsonby, could you go back and find the puppy for us? You see, we know who her owner is, and she's coming here any minute.'

'Then I shall give her a severe talking to!' Mrs Ponsonby retorted. 'It's quite ridiculous, letting these young dogs cavort about all over London. What can she be thinking of?'

'It's a long story,' Mandy said, 'but it really isn't her fault. She's Laura Dawson, a famous writer, and she's so worried about her puppy. Just imagine how you'd feel if Pandora or Toby got lost.'

'You're the only one of us who can get into the Palace gardens, Mrs Ponsonby,' James added. 'Please say you'll help! Laura Dawson will be so grateful.'

Mrs Ponsonby thought it over. 'I will help you,' she said eventually, 'for the sake of the puppy. And because I am aware that duty goes hand in hand with privilege. Luckily, I still have Pandora's lead in my bag. Wait for me here. I shall return!'

'Well!' said Casey, wide-eyed, as Mrs Ponsonby and her feathers sailed away. 'She is something else!'

'Has there been any news?' Laura Dawson said, rushing up to Mandy, James and Casey as they waited in a huddle on the pavement. 'Have you seen your friend? And what are you doing on your own? Where's your father?'

'Princess is in the Palace gardens!' Mandy told her excitedly. 'Mrs Ponsonby saw her there. She's gone back in to see whether she can get her out, but it's been about twenty minutes and there's no sign of her yet. Oh, and Dad's in the park with everyone else. They should all be coming back here any minute.'

'How wonderful!' Laura exclaimed. 'That means we're nearly there. George and Henry are safe at home, just round the corner. If only this Mrs Ponsonby can rescue Princess, they'll all be together again! I can't dare to hope . . .'

'She's a bit of a dragon,' Casey warned her. 'She might give you her views on puppies running around without collars.'

'Oh, I don't mind that,' Laura said with a sigh. 'It'll be worth it to have Princess back. And besides, in a way she's right. I know I should have had the puppies microchipped, in case something like this happened. I'm going to make an appointment with the vet straightaway.'

'Good idea,' said Mandy. 'It is worth it, and it won't hurt them at all.'

Casey broke into their conversation. 'There's Mum and Dad!' she said, pointing across the road. 'And your parents, too – and all the others. Looks like they've had enough of waiting for us.'

'Any luck?' Emily Hope said, as they all met on the pavement. 'We really should be making a move now, Mandy.'

'Oh, Mum, Dad! We're almost there!' Mandy said urgently. 'Mrs Ponsonby's seen Princess, and she's gone back inside the Palace gardens to find her. Please, we have to wait until she comes out again!'

Hurriedly, she introduced Laura Dawson to everyone before turning back to search for any sign of Mrs Ponsonby coming out of the side gate.

'We've heard all about the puppies,' Mandy's gran put in. 'But the thing is, we all have presents to buy before we go back to Welford tomorrow. Why don't we give Mrs Ponsonby a ring tonight to find out what happened?'

'I'm perfectly happy to stay here on my own,' Laura Dawson added. 'You've all done so much already.'

'Oh, please – can't we wait a little longer?' Mandy pleaded. 'This may be the only chance we have to see Princess.' She just couldn't bear the thought of leaving the Palace without knowing whether the last puppy had been found.

'I know!' James said. 'Why don't you go shopping here, in the Queen's Gallery next to the Royal Mews? Don't you remember, Mandy? We called in there on Monday.'

'Of course!' Mandy seized on the idea eagerly. 'They sell all kinds of things there – books, china and glass, and chocolates and biscuits with Buckingham Palace on. And model soldiers, too. Your great-grandson Tommy would like those, Mr Pickard.'

'That sounds perfect,' Adam Hope said. 'Nice and close by, and we can get all our shopping done in one fell swoop.'

So it was all agreed. Everyone who wanted to shop went off to the Queen's Gallery, and Mandy, James and Casey had another half-hour to wait with Laura for news of Princess.

'Oh, come on, Mrs Ponsonby,' Mandy muttered under her breath. 'Do your best!' What was happening behind those tall iron railings? Had Princess run off again? Had she been taken somewhere else?

Another fifteen minutes passed as they all waited anxiously, too tense to talk much. And then at last, Casey let out a cheer. 'I spy the hat!' she shouted. 'There she is!'

Behind the tall railings, the pink and purple feathers of Mrs Ponsonby's hat seemed to shine triumphantly as she advanced towards them. A Palace official opened the gate to let her through.

'Is Princess with her?' Mandy called urgently. 'Can anyone see?'

'Yes, she is!' Casey shouted, throwing her baseball cap in the air. 'Oh, good old Mrs Ponsonby! She's done it!'

'Princess!' Laura Dawson called, crouching down and throwing her arms wide open. 'Come on, girl!'

Mrs Ponsonby bent down to slip Pandora's lead from round Princess's neck. And then, in a streak of brown fur, the last little chocolate Labrador puppy came bounding across the pavement towards her owner.

'Oh, thank you, Mrs Ponsonby!' Mandy cried, taking her hand and pumping it up and down in her excitement. 'Thank you for finding Princess. How did you do it?'

'I applied my knowledge of dog psychology,' Mrs Ponsonby said modestly. 'And then I tempted her out with a ham sandwich.'

'I'm so grateful to you all,' Laura said, smiling as broadly as Princess. She buckled the puppy's collar and clipped on her lead before standing up, the puppy in her arms. 'If you won't accept any reward, then I insist on taking you all out, just as soon as Princess is safely back home. How about tea at the Ritz Hotel?'

'Tea at the Ritz!' Casey said, her eyes shining. 'This day is just getting better and better. Wait 'til I tell Mom and Dad!'

Mandy gave Princess a hug, and the little dog licked her hand. She looked thin and dirty, but otherwise, she seemed to be fine. 'So what have you been up to inside Buckingham Palace?' Mandy asked, taking the puppy's head in her hands and gazing into her beautiful brown eyes. Then she turned to Laura Dawson. 'You ought to write about Princess's adventures in your next book,' she said. 'They'd make a great story.'

Laura Dawson laughed. 'Come on, Mandy!' she replied. 'A pup at the Palace? Now who'd believe that?'

Dog
at the
Door

One

It was Hallowe'en; Mandy Hope had been to a fancy dress party in the village hall and now, as she hurried down the lane towards Animal Ark, she was remembering all the ghosts and skeletons and other creepy things she'd seen! She'd passed the row of cottages behind the Fox and Goose where reassuring lights glowed from behind closed curtains. But the moon had just gone behind a cloud.

Mandy shivered and wished she'd agreed to her best friend, James Hunter, walking home with her. She blinked to get used to the darkness, then peered ahead. Something stealthily moved out of the ditch at one side of the lane. She gasped and faltered to a standstill as it came creeping towards her.

Then she smiled and crouched down, holding a hand out in front of her. 'Jet! What are you up to? You nearly frightened the life out of me!'

The little black cat miaowed and came eagerly towards her. As Mandy picked her up, she heard light footsteps and found herself caught in the beam of a torch.

'Mandy! You look really frightening in that outfit!' said Elise Knight, laughing. Elise lived in one of the cottages Mandy had just passed.

'I'm the wicked witch of Welford!' Mandy whispered in a low, deep voice. 'I should have borrowed Jet,' she added with a chuckle. 'She'd have made a fantastic witch's cat!'

'She's just been for a walk with me and Maisy,' explained Elise. 'She comes with us every evening now. Although sometimes she doesn't stick so close.'

'Well, she gave me a real fright!' said Mandy. She put the little black cat down, so she could pet Maisy, Elise's Dalmatian. 'She suddenly appeared from the ditch. All I could see was a weird black shape creeping towards me!'

'Quite brave of her coming up to you in that get-up!' said Elise. 'I'd have thought seeing that broom would have made her turn tail and run.'

'It's Grandad's garden brush,' said Mandy. 'I think it helped me win a prize for my costume. But the others looked great too! I left them at the end of the lane. They've gone off to trick or treat round the village.'

'I'd better get off home so I can have a few treats ready in case they come knocking on my door,' said Elise. 'I don't fancy anyone playing any tricks on me!'

'And I've got to hurry too, so I can have supper ready for Mum when she comes home,' said Mandy. 'She's been at a veterinary convention in York all day.'

Mandy walked her fingers across Maisy's nose. Maisy was deaf and had been trained to recognise hand-signals. This one was Mandy's special way of saying 'goodbye' to the Dalmatian.

Only the dim night-lights were on in Animal Ark's surgery, a modern extension built on to the back of the old stone cottage where the Hope family lived. Mandy walked along the side of the building to go in the front entrance.

As she went round the corner, she thought she heard a rustling noise in the rhododendron bush. She couldn't see anything and she didn't hear the noise again. But she still got herself inside as quickly as she could.

The sound of music drifted round the small

hallway. It was coming from upstairs. Mandy was glad. That meant her dad hadn't been called out. He'd be lying on the bed resting his sore ankle and maybe reading *Veterinary News* while he listened to the radio. He'd been up all the previous night with Duke, Dan Venables' Shire horse, who'd had a nasty bout of colic. In his distress, poor Duke had kicked out at Mr Hope and caught him on his ankle bone.

Mandy went upstairs and popped her head round the door to tell her dad she was home, but Mr Hope was fast asleep with his sore ankle propped up on a pillow, and his magazine lying open on the bed beside him. Mandy smiled and went to get out of her fancy-dress costume.

Before long, she had supper all organised. The soup she'd taken from the fridge was heating gently in the pan on the Aga and there were cheese sandwiches all ready to grill.

'Now all we need is Mum!' Mandy murmured to herself. 'It's eight o'clock; she said any time between eight and eight-thirty.' Then she frowned. Had she heard a knock at the front door, or not? It wouldn't be her mum, she'd have used her key.

There it was again. Not a knock exactly, more of a muffled thump.

'It must be trick or treaters!' said Mandy as the thumping became more persistent. 'All right, I'm coming,' she called. She picked up a handful of treacle toffees to offer as a treat and went to the door.

But when she opened the door, Mandy felt her smile fade and her eyes widen in disbelief. A distraught and panting Golden Retriever was straining at its lead, trying to reach the door. The end of the lead had been looped through the fancy wrought-iron whirls of one of their plant containers and the dog couldn't get it loose.

When the dog saw Mandy it whined and strained harder at the lead, dragging the plant-pot along with a series of thumps. *So that's what I heard*, thought Mandy, stepping quickly forward.

'It's all right, everything's going to be all right.' Her voice was quiet and soothing as she bent down in front of the dog.

She let it sniff her hand before stroking its soft golden head. The dog was still whimpering but it had stopped straining quite so hard at the lead and was gazing at Mandy with imploring eyes.

'Don't worry. I'm going to unfasten you. I can't do it from here, the lead's pulling too tight. Just hang on a minute, I'll have to move round behind you.'

Mandy straightened up slowly; any sudden movement would make the dog even more scared.

She placed her hands carefully around the dog's body so she could unclip the lead from its collar.

Mandy bit her lip as she realised the dog was pregnant. She often helped her parents in the surgery and sometimes went on home visits with one or other of them. She'd seen and handled quite a few dogs who were having puppies so she knew the signs. And, from the feel of things, this poor Golden Retriever was very pregnant; her sides were rounded like a barrel and her tummy felt low and droopy. Mandy was a bit worried about trying to move her on her own.

But the dog suddenly stepped backwards, releasing the tension on the lead. 'Good girl! Clever girl! I can manage now! That's right, just keep still for a second,' said Mandy.

After two or three attempts, Mandy managed to move the tiny knob on the clasp of the collar and release the metal ring. 'There,' she breathed at last. 'I've done it.'

The dog sat down and Mandy ran her free hand over the dog's plump side. 'Come on,' she persuaded. 'We're going indoors.' The dog struggled to her feet. 'There's a good girl,' praised Mandy. 'Come on.' The dog whined heart-breakingly and pulled in the opposite direction to the door.

Mandy's heart lurched; the poor dog sounded so

distressed, but she knew the sooner she got her in and tried to calm her, the better it would be.

'No! *This* way,' she said in a firmer tone, giving the collar a sharp tug. Mandy heaved a sigh of relief as the dog suddenly decided to stop struggling and allowed herself to be taken inside.

Mandy kicked the front door shut behind them and led the dog down the hall and into the kitchen. She shut the kitchen door too. She had a feeling the dog would want to try and get away again.

Mandy walked the dog over towards the Aga. 'You sit here,' Mandy tapped the floor in front of the warm stove. 'I want to see if there's a name tag on your collar. It would be much better if I knew what to call you, wouldn't it, girl?'

To Mandy's surprise the dog sat down. There was no name tag, but Mandy did notice a triangle of black on the dog's creamy-gold chest. 'That's an unusual mark,' Mandy told the dog. 'It might help in finding out who you belong to. But you do need a name; I'll call you Goldie. Now, I'm going to warm you a drop of milk, then I'll go and wake Dad.'

As soon as Mandy let go of her collar, Goldie started to wander round the kitchen sniffing in corners and under the table and round the chairs. Then she started whimpering and whining as she scrabbled at the stone floor.

Mandy couldn't bear it! She knelt down in front of the dog and took hold of her front paws. 'Don't do that, Goldie,' she begged. 'Everything will be all right, I'm sure it will.' The dog whined and licked Mandy's hand. But then she pulled her paws free and began to scrabble again.

'I'm going for Dad *now*,' said Mandy. She didn't want to leave the dog alone, but she knew she had to get help.

Mandy started to get up; the dog stopped scrabbling at the floor, whined louder and harder and banged her head against Mandy's tummy.

'Oh, Goldie! I only want to leave you for a minute,' said Mandy, trying to hold the dog's head still. 'I've got to go and get some help. Dad might be able to give you something to calm you down a bit.'

The dog let her head lie in Mandy's hands. But the look in her eyes was such a lost, bewildered, *hurting* look, Mandy couldn't bring herself to try and get up again. 'We'll just have to sit here like this till Mum comes home or Dad wakes up,' she said and she thought she saw the dog's tail wag ever so slightly.

Then Mandy heard the sharp, shrill sound of the telephone. It only rang twice and Mandy let out a long breath. Her dad might be able to sleep with the radio playing, but the telephone ringing always woke him instantly.

Sure enough, a couple of minutes later, the kitchen door opened and Adam Hope came in. 'So it wasn't a hoax call!' he said, shaking his head. 'Somebody just phoned to ask if we'd found a dog at the door,' he added. And he walked slowly to where Mandy was kneeling with the Golden Retriever's head in her lap.

</>

Two

Two

As Mr Hope drew closer, the dog began to tremble and tried to wriggle herself even closer to Mandy. 'She's really upset, Dad. I was going to come and fetch you but she got herself into such a state, I was scared to leave her.'

Mr Hope nodded. 'Keep talking, Mandy. If she realises me being here isn't worrying you, she might accept it too.'

Mandy stroked the dog's head and face with gentle fingers. 'It's all right, Goldie,' she said quietly. 'We're going to help you.' Mandy was still kneeling back on her heels and she wished she could move into a more comfortable position.

But the dog whined and kept wriggling; by now

her chest and most of the front of her body was over Mandy's legs. 'Keep still, there's a good girl,' Mandy pleaded. 'You might damage your puppies, wriggling like this. There, that's better, that's right, nice and still. And you've stopped trembling, haven't you! Are you going to make friends with Dad now?'

'Puppies?' whispered Mr Hope, crouching down beside them.

'I think she's a good few weeks pregnant, Dad.' Mandy gulped. 'She was tied up to one of the heavy plant pots and she was dragging it along behind her, trying to reach the door.'

Mr Hope looked grim but his voice was gentle and reassuring as he spoke to the dog. 'Hello, girl. There's a good dog, come on, let me have a look at you.'

The dog looked at the hand he was holding out, then raised her head to look up at Mandy.

'It's OK, Goldie. Let Dad check you over.' Mandy took Mr Hope's hand in hers and drew it closer to the dog's face. 'There, see, that's it . . . you're letting him stroke you now . . . there's a clever girl.'

'I don't suppose there was an address on the name tag?' Mr Hope asked as he ran his hands over the dog's back and sides.

'There isn't a name tag,' Mandy shook her head. 'I just had to call her something. I don't know why, it didn't seem right saying 'dog' or 'girl' all the time.

Not when she was feeling so alone. And, who—'

Mandy forced herself to stop talking. She wanted to ask 'who could have done a thing like this?' But she knew the anger would have shown in her voice and that would have worried the poor animal even more. Instead, she watched with anxious eyes while Mr Hope continued to run his hands over the dog.

'Her abdomen is very saggy,' he said, glancing up at Mandy. 'You're right, love, she is pregnant. In fact,' he stroked his beard thoughtfully, 'I think the pups are due near enough any day now. I'll need to give her a more thorough examination. But for now . . . has she had anything to drink?'

'I got the milk out of the fridge, but that's as far as I got,' Mandy told him. She sighed with relief as the dog moved off her legs.

'Don't move too far away from her,' said Mr Hope. 'She's calmed down quite a lot, her breathing's not so panicky. I'll warm some milk and bring it over.'

Mr Hope placed the bowl of milk in front of her a few minutes later. At first, the dog just stared at it. Then Mandy saw her lick her lips and she held her breath as Goldie got to her feet. But she just sniffed at the bowl and then turned her head to gaze at Mandy with reproachful eyes.

'What's the matter, girl? Don't you like milk? Perhaps she wants water, Dad? I think she wants *something.*'

But the Golden Retriever didn't even bother to sniff at the bowl of water when it was offered.

'How about tea?' Mandy asked. 'Flo Maynard's Butch drinks tea. Or what about sweetening the milk with glucose?'

Mr Hope smiled and nodded. 'Just what I was about to suggest,' he said.

'Well, she's not over-enthusiastic but at least she's drinking it,' said Mandy, after her dad had added some glucose solution to the milk.

As they watched the dog slowly lapping, Mandy asked her dad about the phone call.

'I'm almost sure it was from a call box,' said Mr Hope. 'I could hear traffic in the background. It was a lady and she sounded upset, but she only asked if we'd found a dog at the door before hanging up.'

'Do you think Goldie's *her* dog? Do you think she abandoned her? Or could she have *stolen* Goldie and panicked when she realised she had a pregnant dog on her hands?'

Mr Hope didn't have time to answer. Goldie suddenly lifted her head from the bowl and stared intently towards the door.

'That'll be Mum!' said Mandy, moving swiftly. 'I'd better warn her to come in quietly.' She intercepted her mum at the door and explained the situation.

'I can't leave you two alone for a second, can I?' Emily Hope was shrugging off her outdoor coat as she spoke. She wasn't looking at her daughter or her husband; her green eyes were on the dog.

Mandy caught her father's gaze. The Golden Retriever hadn't moved, but she was looking at Mrs Hope and her long, plumed tail was moving ever so slightly.

'Are you coming to say hello, then?' Mrs Hope stayed where she was, crouched down and held her hand out. 'I want to see if *she'll* come to *me*,' she said quietly. 'Do we know her name?'

'I call her Goldie,' Mandy replied.

'I don't think your mum's going to have to call her anything,' Mr Hope whispered.

Mandy nodded and smiled. The dog was padding slowly but surely towards Emily Hope.

'She's a beauty,' said Mrs Hope. 'Well cared for, too, from the look of her. But she's worried and disorientated, aren't you, girl! You're with strangers and there's no familiar smells, or toys, or bedding box for you. Poor Goldie.'

'I don't think Goldie really *is* her name,' said Mandy.

'It will do for now.' Mrs Hope was still concentrating on the dog, who was moving closer and closer.

Mandy held her breath as she watched to see what would happen. When Goldie reached Emily Hope, she sat down. Then, with her head slightly to one side, she lifted a paw.

Mandy felt a great big lump in her throat while she watched the two of them. The dog's brown eyes held such a sad look as she sat there with her paw trustingly in Mrs Hope's hand. They stayed like that for a few seconds, then Goldie withdrew her paw and stood up. She looked over towards Mandy and Adam Hope before padding over to them.

'An encouraging sign,' murmured Mr Hope. 'Don't move yet, Mandy. Let the dog play it her way.'

This time the dog gave a little grunt as she sat

down and held up a paw. She was looking at Mr Hope so he stepped forward first.

'Still wary of me, aren't you, girl!' he murmured, noting the slight trembling and the speed at which the Retriever withdrew her paw. 'I don't think she's used to men,' he added, glancing at his wife as he moved away.

'Mmm, she definitely seems to relate better to females.' A small smile touched Emily Hope's lips as Goldie shuffled, still sitting, a couple of centimetres closer to Mandy.

Mandy knelt down in front of Goldie before taking her paw. She was pleased to see the dog's eyes were starting to lose their hurt expression. 'She must be feeling safer with us now,' said Mandy, using her free hand to play gently with the soft fur on Goldie's chest.

'She needs a closer examination than the one I gave her,' said Mr Hope. 'And we need to check to see if she's been micro-chipped.'

Mandy knew that a lot of owners had a numbered micro-chip injected painlessly into their pet's neck. Most vets, police stations and branches of the RSPCA had a special scanner they could use to reveal the number. 'I hadn't got round to thinking of that!' said Mandy. 'If Goldie *has* been micro-chipped someone will be able to trace her owner, won't they?'

Mrs Hope nodded. 'Either way, we'll have to inform all the authorities as soon as we know. I think it would be best if you and I handled her, Mandy. Let's see if we can get her to come through to the surgery.'

'You could finish off supper, Dad,' said Mandy. 'The sandwiches are all ready to toast. Poor Mum must be starving!'

'I am,' agreed Mrs Hope. 'But as always it's—'

'Animals first!' laughed Mandy and Adam Hope together.

'No micro-chip,' reported Mrs Hope, after she'd run the scanner over Goldie's neck. 'And no name on her collar either. Put it back on, Mandy, then you can hold her steady while I listen to her heart and lungs.'

Mandy watched Mrs Hope's expression carefully and smiled when her mother gave a satisfied nod. 'No problems there,' she said. 'Ears, eyes, mouth and nose are fine, too. I think she's about eighteen months old. And this is probably her first pregnancy.

'Her nails feel naturally short . . .' Mandy leaned over to feel for herself and Mrs Hope continued, '. . . so it seems as though she's used to walking on pavements or rough tracks. Indoor dogs, or ones who only have a garden for exercising in, usually need their nails trimming with clippers.'

'Goldie's turned out to be a good name for her,' chuckled Mandy. 'She's being as good as gold. She doesn't seem to mind being up on the examination table at all!'

'Not up till now,' Mrs Hope smiled and reached for a pair of rubber gloves from the trolley. 'She might not be so happy at this next bit though. Hold her tail up, Mandy. I want to take her temperature.'

Mandy watched as her mother greased the snub-nosed end of a glass thermometer, then spoke soothingly to Goldie as it was gently inserted. The dog flinched a bit but she didn't struggle. 'There, I'm proud of you,' Mandy whispered.

'It won't take long, girl,' murmured Mrs Hope.

'Is her temperature OK?' asked Mandy, half a minute or so later when her mother removed the thermometer.

'Slightly below normal, just a little over thirty-seven.'

'Is that something to worry about, Mum?'

'Not in the way you mean, love. A normal temperature is around thirty-eight or thirty-nine. But in a pregnant dog, a dropping temperature is one of the signs that the pups are within a day or two of being born.'

'Dad thought they were due near enough any day,'

said Mandy, as she helped Mrs Hope lift the heavy dog from the table to the floor. 'What are we going to do, Mum? What if nobody's reported her missing? Where will she go to have her pups?'

Mrs Hope took a lead from the hook on the door and clipped it on to the dog's collar before replying. 'One thing at a time, Mandy. We'll take some food through with us. You can make her a meal while Dad and I sort a few things out. Come on, girl,' she added, patting the top of her leg to encourage the dog to follow her.

She passed Mandy a tin of special care dog food and a packet of biscuit meal from the display in the reception area and the three of them walked through the connecting door back into the kitchen. But Goldie whined anxiously and pulled towards the back door.

'Shall I take her into the garden, Mum?' Mandy asked. 'I'll keep her lead on but she can't get out anyway. The gate's shut; I came in that way.'

'Yes. Keep a good hold of the lead, though I don't think she'll try to run off; I think she just wants to relieve herself after having her tummy felt. Leave the door open and call out if you need any help.'

Sniffing here and there, the Golden Retriever padded round the garden for a while before crouching down. 'Good girl,' praised Mandy. 'Shall we go back in now and get you something to eat?'

Goldie seemed only too anxious to go back inside. And when Mandy unclipped the lead she made straight for the spot in front of the stove.

Mrs Hope was munching a raw carrot. 'Just something to hold hunger at bay,' she said. 'Your dad's gone to make a few phone calls. The kettle's boiled and I've put some yeast extract in that jug. You can make some gravy to soak the biscuit meal in.'

'How much of everything?' Mandy asked.

'Just soak a very small handful of the biscuit meal. Then mix it with a quarter of the tinned meat.'

'Are we not giving her much in case the food doesn't agree with her, Mum?'

Emily Hope smiled. 'That would be a reason, normally. But even if we knew what Goldie's usual diet was, we'd still only give her a small portion to prevent her from feeling bloated. At this stage of pregnancy it's best to feed a dog little and often, rather than giving her one or two main-sized meals. And it wouldn't surprise me if Goldie didn't want anything to eat at all.'

'Because she's in a strange place, Mum?'

'That could be a reason, of course. But refusing food is another sign that the pups are only a day or two away from being born.' Mrs Hope smiled. 'We'll see what happens when you offer her some.'

'Who's Dad phoning?' asked Mandy as she opened the tin.

'The police, the dog warden, the RSPCA, Betty Hilder and the Golden Retriever Rescue,' Mrs Hope smiled. 'Though, unless it was a dog thief with an attack of guilty conscience who phoned, which is extremely unlikely, I very much doubt there'll be any report of a missing Golden Retriever that matches the description of this lass.'

'What comes next, then?' asked Mandy. She carried on mixing the dog food, but turned her head to look down at Goldie. The dog was lying on one side, her body slightly curled and her legs stretched out. She'd crossed one front paw over the other, her head was resting on the floor and she was watching Mandy.

Mandy stopped what she was doing and kneeled down beside the dog. Goldie licked Mandy's hand and gave a little whine.

I just hope that nobody's coming to take her away to the dog pound, thought Mandy, as she played gently with Goldie's ears.

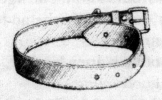

Three

'All arranged,' said Mr Hope. He was limping slightly as he walked back into the kitchen.

'What is?' Mandy asked anxiously.

'Betty Hilder says she could have Goldie and her litter at the animal sanctuary. She thinks she'd probably be able to find homes for the pups when they're old enough. And the Golden Retriever Rescue would be willing to take Goldie. That's unless someone claims her, of course, which I doubt.'

'We won't be taking Goldie to the animal sanctuary tonight, will we, Dad?'

Mr Hope smiled at his daughter. 'No; unless she's claimed, Goldie's staying here to have her pups,' he said.

'That's brilliant!' said Mandy, dashing over to give him a hug. 'Does Mum know? She's gone for a quick shower. What's the matter?' she added as her dad gave a small gasp.

'You put me off balance a bit, love, and my ankle isn't feeling so good.'

'Oh, Dad! I'd forgotten all about Duke kicking you. Tell you what . . .'

Mandy reached the first-aid box down, then handed Mr Hope a tub of soothing cream. 'Sit down and rub some of this on your ankle while I dish up supper.' She turned to glance over at the Golden Retriever. 'I don't think Goldie wants hers.'

'Don't worry about it, Mandy. Expectant mums often go off their food a couple of days before the pups are due.'

Mandy nodded. 'That's what Mum said. But I'm worried in case she feels too strange and unhappy to eat.'

'Well, we'll see how things develop. In the meantime, let's try and make sure she takes a reasonable amount of fluid.'

Adam Hope gave a little groan as he started to rub the cream in and, immediately, Goldie waddled over to him. She sniffed at his ankle, then, whining a little as though in sympathy, she licked his hand.

'Well, I don't know whether you're sorry for me

or if you just like the smell of the cream,' Mr Hope said softly. 'But you're a good, brave girl, aren't you!'

'She's thanking you for letting her stay to have her pups,' said Mandy. She smiled as Goldie allowed Mr Hope to rub the top of her golden head before turning to waddle away. 'Dad, do you think her owner *did* abandon her? How could anyone bear to? She's such a loving, gentle animal!'

'She's also having puppies,' Mr Hope replied grimly. 'Maybe her owner hadn't bargained for that!'

'But they'd have noticed before now!' said Mandy. 'I think she was stolen and the thieves panicked when they realised she was pregnant.'

'In that case, she'll be reported missing.' Mr Hope shook his head. 'Only time will tell, Mandy.'

Mandy nodded. 'Look, she's settling down in front of the stove again. I'll get my big bean-bag for her later. We can put an old blanket and a sheet over it. And what about—'

'Mandy! Supper?' prompted Adam Hope, smiling. 'I'm sure that soup is more than ready by now and I toasted the sandwiches while you and Mum were examining Goldie. They're on a baking tray in the oven. If we don't get them soon, they'll be soggy.'

'It'll be a bit of a struggle getting them out,' Mandy chuckled. 'There isn't that much room between Goldie and the oven door.'

In the end, Mandy had to kneel down and stretch over the big dog to get the tray of toasted sandwiches out. 'It's all right, just you keep still,' whispered Mandy.

Goldie blinked sleepily then yawned; other than that, she didn't move a muscle.

'That soup smells good!' Emily Hope hurried in looking pink and warm. Mandy hid a grin. Her mum's cheeks were clashing terribly with her red hair which was tied up on top of her head. 'You look pleased, Mandy,' Mrs Hope said. 'I guess that means your dad got the OK for Goldie to stay awhile?'

Mandy nodded and carried the soup bowls to the table.

'What I want to know,' said Mandy, once they were all tucking in, 'is why you're letting Goldie stay at Animal Ark for the next few days? You're usually so strict about not taking in waifs and strays. Not that I'm complaining, of course,' she added with a happy smile.

'Special circumstances,' Mr Hope replied. 'If it's the dog's first litter, and we think it is, she might need help when the pups start to arrive. Especially after what she's been through this evening. Letting her go to another strange place with another lot of strangers, well . . .' Mr Hope shook his head.

'Your dad and I agreed that it would have caused

her too much distress,' said Emily Hope. 'And moving Goldie around could send her into labour before she's completely ready.'

'I think it's unlikely she'll start for a day or two,' said Adam Hope. 'But first thing tomorrow we'll have to organise things. Fix up a proper place for her to have the pups. Try and get her familiar with that place before anything happens.'

'What do you mean, fix up a proper place?' Mandy asked.

Emily Hope smiled. 'It will be easier to keep an eye on her if she's in the house,' she said. 'Besides, she might settle better if she feels part of the family while she's here. Though I think it would be sensible to confine her to the kitchen. It's handy for the garden and it's the best room to arrange a birth area in.'

'I'll phone James first thing in the morning,' Mandy said eagerly. 'He'll be really glad to come and help. That's if you don't think it will upset Goldie seeing another new face?'

'She'll probably feel happy enough about James,' said Mrs Hope. 'Golden Retrievers are popular family dogs because they like having people around them. And she'll be able to smell Blackie on him, which should help.'

Blackie was James Hunter's black Labrador. James

had had him since he was a tiny pup, so he was used to handling dogs. He loved animals almost as much as Mandy did; the two of them had often worked together helping ill or injured animals.

When they'd cleared the supper things away, Mandy fetched the big bean-bag from the corner of her bedroom, as well as a soft old blanket and a sheet. 'This is your bed, girl,' she told the dog. Goldie lifted her head to glance at it, then closed her eyes and went back to sleep.

'Just leave it there. She might decide to use it later,' said Emily Hope. 'And listen, Mandy, I don't want you to keep coming down in the night to check her. I'm sure she won't go into labour just yet, but I'll look in on her a couple of times anyway. All right?'

Mandy knew from her mother's firm tone that she really meant what she said.

'All right,' she agreed. 'But how about if I get up early? I'll take Goldie into the garden if she wants to go and I'll give her some milk afterwards. I can get all my jobs done early as well, then I'll phone James. That would be OK, wouldn't it, Mum?'

'Fine,' Mrs Hope replied and Mandy went happily to bed.

Next morning, James arrived at Animal Ark ten minutes after Mandy had phoned him. She'd told him not to knock on the back door but to come straight in. 'That way, Goldie will think you're one of us,' she'd said.

So James, slightly out of breath and his eyes bright behind his glasses, walked in and went straight over to sit at the kitchen table. 'Dad's changing the front wheel on my bike,' he said. 'I ran all the way here.' James lived at the other end of the village.

At the sound of his voice, the Golden Retriever lifted her head from her paws. She looked at him steadily for a moment, then lowered her head again.

James smiled. 'Not exactly the "big hello", but at least she isn't bothered that I'm here. She's very pretty, Mandy, she's got such a gentle-looking face.'

'She's got a lovely gentle nature too,' said Mandy. 'She really likes it there in front of the stove, James. I took her out in the garden early on, then persuaded her to drink some milk when we came back in. She didn't want any food, but Dad said not to worry about that. After she'd had her milk she went straight back there and lay down. She's completely ignored the bean-bag bed I made for her.'

'She's probably used to lying in front of a range wherever she's come from.' James looked from Goldie to Mandy, a look of disbelief on his face. 'Do you think she *has* been abandoned, Mandy?'

Mandy shrugged helplessly. 'Dad's phoned all the

places he contacted last night and there's still no report of a Golden Retriever missing from home,' she said. 'But if she was stolen, it might have been miles out of our area.'

James scowled and shook his head. 'It doesn't take long for details to be circulated to other areas,' he pointed out. 'They'll use computers to do that.'

'Well, all we can do is to make her feel as good as possible,' said Mandy. 'And to fix up a special place for when she has the puppies.'

'I've been thinking about that!' Adam Hope came in just in time to hear Mandy's last words. He smiled a greeting to James, then pointed to a large double cupboard under the work surface, a couple of metres away from the stove.

'We could pull that out. I'm sure we can find somewhere else to put it temporarily. And I reckon one of those specially designed whelping boxes would fit perfectly in the space. The single cupboard will separate it from the stove, so that area will be nice and warm without being too hot.'

'Have we got a spare whelping box in the surgery?' Mandy asked.

'No. We need to keep ours in case of any emergencies. But, luckily,' Mr Hope grinned, 'the rep who works for the firm that makes them lives in Walton.'

Walton was only two miles away from Welford;

Mandy and James went to Walton Moor School there. They weren't in the same class; James was a year younger than Mandy.

'I've already phoned him,' Mr Hope continued. 'He's agreed to bring his sample model over. All we need to do is assemble it.'

'Dad! You're brilliant!' said Mandy. 'Come on, James, help me drag the cupboard out!'

'Er, Mandy,' James shoved his glasses further on to his nose, 'doesn't your mum keep crockery in that cupboard?'

'Yes, but . . . Oh, I see what you're getting at!' Mandy laughed. 'You're right, James. We'll have to empty it first!'

'That's down to you two,' said Mr Hope, ruffling Mandy's hair. 'I've done my bit for now. I've got to make a couple of home visits. One of them's to Yindee. *Another* tummy upset!'

Mandy chuckled. Yindee was a Siamese cat with a habit of eating wool. No matter how hard her owner tried to hide woollen jumpers and cardigans from the Siamese, Yindee somehow managed to find every new hiding place. She'd claw at the garment until the wool started to unravel, then bite off and eat all the loose bits.

'Make sure you keep your jacket on while you're there, Dad!' Mandy glanced meaningfully at the warm, woollen jumper Adam Hope was wearing.

'Will do,' he replied cheerfully. 'Hello, girl,' he added softly. Goldie had raised her head again and was looking at him. 'Do you want a pat, then? Have you decided I'm not too bad after all?'

'She wasn't sure of Dad at first,' Mandy told James, as they watched Mr Hope stroking the dog.

'I bet she soon came round though,' said James. 'Both your parents are terrific with animals!'

As Mandy nodded, she noticed that Mr Hope's hands were moving slowly over Goldie's barrel-like sides.

'Everything *is* OK, isn't it, Dad?' she whispered anxiously.

'As far as I can tell, everything seems fine, love. Just make sure you take her outside as soon as she shows any sign of wanting to go. The pups will be pushing against her bladder, so she'll need to relieve herself quite often.'

'OK,' said Mandy. 'We'll empty the cupboard and see if she wants to go out before we start moving it.' She smiled as Goldie pawed at James's trainers.

A look of delight appeared on her friend's face and he bent down to stroke the dog. Mandy guessed he'd been longing to do that, but James was good with animals, too; he'd known to wait until Goldie *wanted* him to pet her.

* * *

By the time Desmond Barratt, the sales representative, arrived at the back door with the whelping box, Mandy and James had finished preparing the small area it was to go in.

'I won't come in, Mandy,' Desmond said quietly. 'It might upset the poor lass seeing another stranger. The box is easy enough to assemble; everything slides or slots into place. There's an instruction sheet anyway so you shouldn't have any trouble.'

Before long, the parts of the box were spread out over the kitchen floor. Mandy and James were on their knees, poring over the instruction sheet when Goldie got up and padded towards them.

'You know, Mandy,' James said thoughtfully. 'That leather collar looks awfully heavy for her to wear all the time.'

'You're right, it does!' Mandy got up. 'I'll pop through to the surgery and get a lightweight one for her.'

Jean Knox, Animal Ark's receptionist, glanced up when Mandy hurried through the connecting door. She knew all about Goldie, of course. If anyone happened to phone about the Golden Retriever during surgery hours, she'd be the one to answer the phone. 'Everything OK?' she asked. 'No problems? Your mum's with a patient but I could

get Simon for you.' Simon was the practice nurse.

'No, no problems, Jean,' Mandy assured her. 'But Goldie's wearing a heavy collar. She could do with a lightweight one. Will it be OK if I take one from the sales display?'

'I'll buy it for her, Mandy. I'd like to do something to help.'

'Thanks, Jean,' Mandy smiled. 'I'll tell Goldie that it's a present from you. I'll have a blue one, please.'

Mandy hurried back to the kitchen with the new collar and showed it to Goldie. 'This will be comfier for you,' she said. 'You owe James and Jean a lick!'

Mandy removed the leather collar and put it on the floor beside her. Then she put the new one round the dog's neck. Goldie whined and padded slowly towards the back door.

'You take her, Mandy,' said James. 'I think I've worked out where everything goes and it'll be easier putting it together with Goldie out of the way. She was getting quite interested in all the different pieces while you were gone. Kept snuffling at them.'

'That's good!' said Mandy as she opened the back door. 'Let's hope that means she'll be happy to use it when it's ready.'

Goldie made her way to the end of the garden and squatted down in the place she'd used previously. 'Good girl,' Mandy told her. 'You're starting to make a nice little routine for yourself, aren't you! How about staying out a while longer? Give James time to put your special box together!'

But James suddenly appeared at the back door. 'Mandy! Mandy!' he called urgently. 'Come here – quick!'

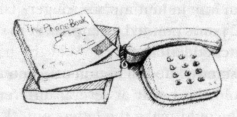

Four

'What's up, James?' Mandy demanded, racing to the back door and turning to wait for Goldie, who was meandering slowly up the path.

'I was picking her leather collar up off the floor and I suddenly thought of examining the underside,' James gabbled quickly.

'Mum and I looked there after we checked to see if she'd been micro-chipped,' Mandy sighed. 'I thought someone had phoned to—'

'Mandy!' James interrupted tersely. 'There *is* a name on it!' He dangled the collar in front of Mandy's eyes. 'I'd never have seen it if I hadn't been looking really closely. I think somebody scratched it on with the point of a needle or something!'

'Where? Let me see!' Mandy almost snatched the collar from him in her impatience.

'There!' James pointed triumphantly to some very faint, scratched lettering.

Mandy screwed up her eyes in concentration; she had to hold the collar at several different angles before she could make the letters out. 'Looks like K . . . I . . . M . . . S . . . L . . . E . . . I . . . O,' she said doubtfully. 'That doesn't sound like a name!'

'I don't think the last two are letters, I think they're numbers!' James told her. 'There's a gap after the E; maybe somebody was going to scratch the address on as well. And it isn't an S there, it's a B! Whoops!' he added as the Golden Retriever nudged his legs with her nose. 'Sorry girl, are we in your way?' James moved aside to allow her to amble through the door.

'B,' said Mandy. 'That would make it . . .' Mandy worked it out. '. . . Kimble!' she said. 'Wow, James! You're a genius!' Mandy just managed to stop herself from hugging him; James got embarrassed so easily!

'There's a Jessica Kimble in the first year at school, isn't there?' Mandy went on excitedly. 'Her dad breeds budgies and I'm sure they haven't got a dog. But it's quite an unusual name. She might have a relation who has. We could phone and ask! She lives in Walton.'

'That's what I thought!' James nodded. 'And if

she hasn't, we can look for Kimbles in the phone book!'

'Keep an eye on Goldie,' said Mandy. 'I'll go and tell Mum about your brilliant discovery and I'll get the phone books. I'll bring all of them, in case we need them. We've got one for every separate area in North Yorkshire!'

'Well, I'm glad it's a fairly uncommon name,' James murmured to Goldie. 'Hey, no, come away from there, girl. I've still got the front bit and one of the side bits to put in place!'

The dog had made for the partly assembled whelping box and looked as if she was about to try and get into it. James knelt down and rubbed his face against the soft fur on the Retriever's chest. She whined, and when James lifted his face, she licked his cheek.

'Oh, Goldie!' James had to take his glasses off and give them a good rub.

Mandy seemed to be taking her time so, with the Golden Retriever watching his every move, James finished assembling the box. 'We should let Mr or Mrs Hope check it before you get in,' he said. 'I'll lift it on to the table for now.'

Goldie watched him with mournful eyes and James swallowed hard. The dog looked so sad!

'Sorry to have been so long, James.' Mandy

returned, carrying four telephone directories. 'Mum phoned Jessica's dad; he's one of our clients. They haven't got any Kimble relations in this part of the country, so it's down to searching for ourselves. Mum said to start checking in the local directory,' she told James. 'But she doesn't want us to phone anyone. She says it will be best if she does that. Surgery's finished, so she'll be through soon.'

'Well, the local one only covers places within fifteen miles or so from here. If we don't find the right Kimble in that, I hope she'll phone all the Kimbles in the rest of the county!' James said fiercely as he crouched down next to the dog.

Mandy gazed at him in astonishment. James was usually so calm and even-tempered.

'Sorry,' he muttered, 'I know your mum *will* do that if she has to. It's just that . . .' James buried his face against Goldie's chest again. 'She's such a fantastic dog,' he said in a muffled voice. 'I think she likes the whelping box. She tried to get in it!'

'It looks great, James,' Mandy told him, then she riffled through the pages of the local directory until she came to the Ks. 'There's five entries under Kimble!' she said. 'Two in Walton – but one's Jessica – two in Glisterdale and one in Upper Barnall. So that's four to try. Oh, I do hope Mum isn't long!'

'Impatience should be your middle name!' Emily

Hope spoke from behind her daughter and Mandy turned to grin at her.

'I didn't hear you come in,' she said.

'I'm not surprised. You were too busy talking. Did you say there are four Kimbles to try?'

Mandy nodded as her mum pulled out a chair and sat down. '*If* we happen to find Goldie's owner,' she said, 'I'll have to report to the RSPCA and let them take things over from there.' She smiled and added gently, 'I know you're hoping we'll be able to return Goldie because she was stolen. But if someone claims her, we'll need to be very sure that *is* what happened.'

'You mean if she hadn't really been stolen, the owner might take her back and abandon her somewhere else?' asked James.

'I'm afraid so, James. That's why we'd have to let people who are used to handling this sort of thing deal with it. But now . . .' Mrs Hope got up and went over to the phone.

When Mandy had read out the first number, James got up from the floor where he'd seen sitting with his arm round Goldie, and joined her at the kitchen table. Their eyes were glued to Mrs Hope as she spoke to someone on the other end of the phone. Even though they could only hear one side of the conversation it was obvious that this Kimble didn't know anything about a Golden Retriever, missing or otherwise.

The second call was no good either. Mandy read the third number out. This time, Mrs Hope seemed to be having trouble in making herself understood.

'I'd like to speak to Mr or Mrs Kimble, please,' she repeated. Then she gave the number she'd dialled. 'Yes that number is listed next to the name Kimble. Initial . . .' she glanced at Mandy who told her. 'Initial P', Mrs Hope said into the phone. 'Oh, I see. Yes, well I'm very sorry to have troubled you.'

She replaced the receiver and grimaced at Mandy and James. 'There's no Kimble there and there never has been,' she reported. 'And he doesn't know anyone called Kimble, either. I think he was telling the truth,' she added wryly.

'It must be a misprint,' said Mandy. 'Let's try the last one.'

'The last *local* one!' James corrected.

Goldie had wandered over to the table and plonked herself down in between him and Mandy. James was stroking her but he kept his eyes on Mrs Hope. From the look on her face *this* phone call was more promising.

'You say your son's got a Golden Retriever?' said

Mrs Hope. 'And she went missing three weeks ago? Yes, yes, please, I would!' She reached for the pad and pen next to the phone.

Mandy clutched at James's arm. This could be it! If Goldie had been stolen three weeks ago and the thief hadn't realised the dog was having pups until yesterday . . .

Mrs Hope turned quickly from the phone. 'She's looking up her son's phone number. She can't remember it. I think she's quite old,' she added with a whisper.

Then she said, 'Yes, I'm here, Mrs Kimble!' Mrs Hope started to write.

But Mandy saw her mum's hand falter; saw her shake her head. She glanced quickly at James just as Mrs Hope said, 'Mrs Kimble? Does your son live in *Australia?*'

Emily Hope had recognised the dialling code immediately; the Hopes had done a six-month exchange with a veterinary practice in New South Wales and they still kept in touch with the Munroes at the Mitchell Gap surgery.

'*Australia!* How could *anyone* think that a dog lost in Australia could end up *here!*' Mandy groaned despairingly. She was so disappointed. James let out a huge sigh and reached for one of the other directories.

'Lighten up, you two,' said Mrs Hope. 'Poor Mrs Kimble was only trying to help! I told you she sounded old,' she said, glancing reprovingly at her daughter.

'Sorry, Mum,' said Mandy. 'I suppose at any other time I'd have found it funny,' she admitted. 'But I was so sure we were going to find the right Kimble this time.'

She turned to Goldie. 'Hey, what's the matter, girl? You shouldn't jump up like that, not in your condition!'

Goldie was trying to get her front legs on to Mandy's lap. She was looking intently at Mandy and she was panting slightly; her long pink tongue lolling out at one side of her mouth.

'Maybe she's trying to get to the whelping box,' said James, glancing up. 'She did try to get in it before, Mrs Hope, but I wanted you to check it first to make sure I've done everything right.'

Mrs Hope smiled, 'OK, I'll do that now. But it looks fine, James.'

James blushed, then turned to Mandy and said, 'There's only one Kimble in this directory! I haven't—'

'James!' gasped Mandy. 'Say that again, will you! Just the first bit.'

James threw her a puzzled glance, but he did as

she'd asked. 'There's only one Kimble in this directory,' he said.

Goldie jumped up again. 'I *was* right!' cried Mandy. 'I *knew* I hadn't imagined it! Mum! James! You know what . . . Oh, we've been so stupid and all because of Jessica!'

Mrs Hope and James stared hard at Mandy. What on earth was she talking about?

'We just assumed that Kimble was her owner's *surname* because of Jessica Kimble,' Mandy said. 'But it isn't, is it, girl? It's *your* name. You're called Kimble, aren't you!'

The Golden Retriever gave one quick, sharp bark. Kimble it was!

Five

'I'm afraid you're right, Mandy,' Mrs Hope sighed as she stroked the excited-looking dog. 'All right, lass, calm down, there's a good girl. That's right, you go and have a drink of water.'

'What do you mean, Mum, you're *afraid* I'm right?' Mandy asked. 'I think it's fantastic that we know her proper name.'

'I know what you mean, Mrs Hope,' said James. 'It's good for Kimble, but not so good for us. We're right back to square one. There's no way we can trace her owner now.'

Mandy looked crestfallen. She'd been so pleased when the Golden Retriever had reacted to hearing her real name, she hadn't thought the rest of it out.

But maybe they weren't back to square one. After all . . .

'I'm not so sure, James,' she said after a while. 'We can tell the RSPCA and the police that she's called Kimble. If she's been reported missing her owner would have given the dog's name, too!'

'That's a point, Mandy. I'll phone them now,' Mrs Hope ruffled Mandy's hair.

'And it *is* good that we can call Kimble by her proper name,' said James. 'That could help her settle down better.'

Mandy nodded. 'As soon as Mum's finished on the phone we'll get the whelping box organised for her.'

The box was just over a metre square. It had a floor but no top. The section at the front was lower and hinged so it could be pulled down. Mrs Hope sent Mandy and James through to the surgery to fetch a pile of newspapers for lining the floor of the box.

'Because her pups are so nearly due, we won't give her a blanket or a sheet to lie on,' said Mrs Hope. 'A little while before she goes into labour she'll probably want to make a nest and will start looking for something to tear up. So if the newspapers are there ready for her, she won't get anxious wondering what to use.'

'You look busy,' came a voice from the doorway.

Mandy looked up with a smile. 'Hi, Dad!' she said. 'Is Yindee OK?'

'She managed to open the airing cupboard door this time,' Mr Hope told them. 'She'd chewed a hole about this size . . .' he made a circle with his thumb and index finger, '. . . in one of Mrs Anderson's best Yorkshire wool blankets. I can never be sure if it's eating the wool that upsets the cat's tummy or guilty feelings at what she's done. Mrs Anderson swears Yindee knows when she's been naughty!' Mandy and James laughed.

'It's possible it's some sort of vitamin or mineral deficiency that makes her feel the need to eat wool,' Mr Hope continued. 'More than likely, it's just a habit, but it's as well to check. I've booked her in for tomorrow. We'll run a couple of tests. And now, what's new with Goldie. Anything?'

'Well . . .' Mandy ran over to give him a hug and to tell him the news about the dog's name.

'So it's Kimble, is it?' said Adam Hope, looking across at the Golden Retriever. 'No doubt about that,' he added, laughing, as Kimble thumped her tail on the floor.

'Come and look at the whelping box!' Mandy dragged her father to the table. 'James did all the assembling,' she said. 'We're going to put it in its place now we've lined it.'

'The newspaper will be warm for the pups to lie on, won't it?' said James as he and Mr Hope lifted the box off the table. '*And* easy to change when it gets soiled.'

Mr Hope nodded. 'Yes! Warmth is very important,' he said. 'If we weren't putting the box in such a cosy place, we would have had to cover the open top with a square of wood and a thick blanket, or use an infra red lamp. We'll still have to keep a check on the temperature but I'm almost sure it will be OK without any of those.'

'What should the temperature be, Mr Hope?' asked James; he was always eager to learn.

'Twenty-one degrees is the ideal, James. It very rarely falls below that in here at this time of year with the Aga going.'

The Hopes didn't use the Aga during the summer months, as it made the kitchen much too hot then. Instead, they used a small electric cooker. Mandy, though, was always pleased when the time came to relight the big, friendly stove. She especially loved the cosiness of their kitchen in winter.

As soon as Mr Hope and James moved back from the whelping box, Kimble padded over eagerly. Without hesitation she stepped over the low front part to settle herself with a contented 'gerrumph' on the bed of newspapers.

'Do you think she might have had a bed like this at home?' James wondered aloud.

'Yes, I think that could be the case,' Adam Hope stroked his beard thoughtfully.

Mandy looked at him. 'There really is something strange about the whole thing, Dad!' she said. 'Kimble's obviously been very well looked after; she seems to be used to lots of love and attention, and it looks as though she's been used to a whelping box.'

'Which means her owner must have been preparing for the birth,' James put in. 'I can't believe such a caring owner would abandon her. But . . .'

'But if she was stolen you'd think we'd have heard from her owner by now,' Mandy nodded. 'There was that phone call to make sure we'd found her,' she said. 'That was strange. If it *was* her owner it's a shame she didn't tell you what Kimble likes to eat, Dad! I know you said not to worry about her not eating but maybe she just doesn't like what we're giving her.'

'I called in at Gran's on my way home,' Adam Hope told her. 'She was making steak and kidney pies so I've brought a few chunks of meat home to mince up. Kimble may well be used to a bit of raw meat in her diet. We'll try her on it in a while, but we'll leave her alone when she's settled in her box. Meanwhile, *I'd* eat almost anything that was offered!'

'Cripes!' gasped James. 'I hadn't realised it was so late. I'll have to go, Mandy. Dad and I are going swimming this afternoon, then we're going to visit my aunt. Will you leave a message with Mum if there's any news about Kimble?'

'Of course I will,' Mandy promised. 'But you're not staying at your aunt's, are you, James?' she added anxiously. James sometimes spent a couple of days with his cousins in the school holidays.

'Not this time,' said James.

'So you'll be able to come round tomorrow morning?'

James grinned. 'Nothing could keep me away!' he said.

That's OK then, thought Mandy as she closed the door behind him. *There's something important James and I need to talk about.*

Kimble stayed happily in her box for an hour or so. Then she clambered out and padded over to Mandy. She lay her head on Mandy's knee and wagged her tail.

'Are you trying to tell me something?' Mandy asked, as she played gently with Kimble's soft golden ears. 'Are you hungry? Shall we try you on some of the steak that Dad got for you?'

Mandy mixed the raw mince with a small portion

of tinned food. She decided not to bother adding anything else. If Kimble ate this meal she'd try adding biscuits to the same mix next time.

Kimble ate about half of what Mandy gave her before going to the door and whining to go out.

Mrs Hope was in the garden planting some tulip bulbs. She smiled when Mandy told her that Kimble had eaten a little bit, then suggested that Kimble might like a slow, short walk down the back lane. 'Put her lead on though, Mandy, and if she shows any reluctance to walk, bring her straight back.'

'I'll turn back well before we reach the cottages anyway,' said Mandy. 'She might get over-excited if we meet any of the other animals. We don't want her getting into a fight with Tom!'

Walter Pickard lived in one of the cottages behind the Fox and Goose and he had three cats. The two females, Scraps and Missie, were friendly, gentle creatures, but Tom was big and fierce and thought nothing of taking on any cat or dog he saw.

'Yes, it wouldn't do for Tom to set eyes on her,' Mrs Hope agreed.

Both Mandy and Kimble enjoyed their short walk. October had been a mild month; the trees were still dressed in their glorious autumnal leaves of yellow, orange, russet, copper and crimson. The little green flowers were still blossoming on ivy hedges and

Mandy saw a blackberry bush still full of juicy berries. Perhaps she'd come and pick some for Gran after she'd taken Kimble back.

Kimble didn't seem in any hurry to turn back. She was bumbling happily along, pausing every now and then to snuffle and scrabble in the hedges' undergrowth, her tail moving slowly from side to side.

Watching her, Mandy grew thoughtful again. Who could possibly have left her at the door of Animal Ark, and why? 'I'll find out, Kimble,' she promised aloud. 'I don't know how yet, but James and I will think of some way to do it.'

Six

Mandy and Kimble were in the back garden when James arrived next day. He saw them from over the gate. Mandy had let Kimble off the lead and she was walking slowly along the edge of the flower bed sniffing and scrabbling at every plant and, now and then, whining anxiously.

'Hello, Kimble,' called James. But Kimble didn't even glance towards him. She was too intent on what she was doing.

'You don't look very happy about things, Mandy! Kimble's still OK, isn't she? Your parents haven't changed their minds about her staying here, have they?'

Mandy gave him a weak grin. 'No, they wouldn't

do that. But you're right about me not feeling too happy. Kimble won't settle indoors at all. She'll come in with me but two minutes later she'll be scratching at the door to come out here. She's done everything she needs to, so it isn't that.'

'Maybe she thinks the whelping box is just for sleeping in. Could she be looking for somewhere to have the pups?' James suggested.

'I wouldn't have thought so,' Mandy sighed. 'Mum checked her earlier on and said she didn't think anything was about to happen just yet. But she does keep whining, so I suppose she might be going into labour.'

'Maybe she's pining for her real home and owner, Mandy. She's bound to do that, even with all the love and attention she's getting here. Trouble is, if nobody's phoned it looks as though she *has* been abandoned.'

'Mmm,' Mandy nodded. 'I want to talk to you about that, but I can't concentrate while Kimble's behaving like this. She hasn't made any attempt to get out of the garden. You'd think she would if her mind was on her real home. She just keeps doing that!' Mandy sighed and they both gazed to where Kimble was sniffing and scrabbling.

'Has your mum or dad seen the way she's acting?' James asked.

'No. Mum's been called out and Dad's busy with patients,' said Mandy. 'And I didn't like to leave her while I went into the surgery.'

'I'll go in and see if I can have a word with Simon,' suggested James. 'He might come up with something.'

'That's a good idea, James!' Mandy took her eyes off Kimble to smile at him. James turned slightly red and hurried off in the direction of the surgery.

When Kimble reached the far end of the flower bed, she lifted her head and looked round the rest of the garden. After that she turned and made her way over to Mandy. 'Do you want to go back indoors?' Mandy asked softly.

Kimble whined, then pawed at Mandy's leggings.

'Oh, Kimble, I really don't know *what* you want,' murmured Mandy. The dog moved away and wandered over to the wire run where Mandy's three rabbits played in warm weather. The nights were very cold now so Mandy had moved the hutch into the garage.

Kimble whined, lay down and tried to get her front paws underneath one of the lengths of wood that supported the wire mesh. There was a small mound of hay in one corner of the run. Kimble seemed to be very interested in it.

Mandy picked the hay up – it was only a handful –

and put it between the dog's front paws. Kimble sniffed it urgently, pawed it apart then looked up at Mandy. She looked bewildered, but all Mandy could do was stroke her.

When James came quietly towards them, he was holding a ball, a rubber bone and a rubber ring.

'Simon thinks she could be searching for something to retrieve!' he said.

'Of course!' Mandy sighed. 'Why didn't I think of that! It's in a Retriever's nature to pick things up and take them to their owner as presents! I remember reading about it in one of the books we got off the library van when we were trying to train Blackie.'

James's Labrador was adorable but he wasn't very obedient. James and Mandy often tried to get him to behave better and had read all sorts of books on dog training.

'Let's put each toy in a different place,' said James.

'OK. I'll hide the ring inside that clump of hay. She seemed extra interested in that,' said Mandy.

James didn't hide the bone and the ball; he put them at the edge of the flower bed a few metres apart. He walked back to Kimble, bent down and put his arms round her neck. 'Go fetch me a present, girl,' he whispered into her ear.

One at a time, Kimble fetched the rubber bone,

the ball and the ring and laid them at Mandy's and James's feet. 'Maybe that *was* it!' said James as he stroked Kimble's head. 'Her tail's really wagging, Mandy.'

But the next second, Kimble had returned to the clump of hay. She pawed and sniffed at it, then whined and looked mournfully at Mandy and James.

'I've just remembered something else!' cried Mandy. 'Wait here, James. And you, Kimble.'

Mandy came back with an armful of hay. She hurried to the rabbits' run, kicked it carefully with her foot to tilt it on one side and put the hay down. 'Come on, James. We'll wait by the back door,' she said.

Once they were there she called, 'OK, Kimble. Find them for me, there's a good girl.'

'Find *what?*' James demanded.

'Wait and see,' Mandy said, smiling. 'I'm sure I've sussed it out. Yes . . . yes . . . Look!'

Eyes bright and her tail wagging really hard, Kimble ambled up the garden towards them. She was holding something in her mouth but James couldn't see what.

'Hold your hand out, James,' whispered Mandy.

James shot Mandy a look, but he did as she'd asked.

'Give it to James. Good girl,' Mandy encouraged, and gently and carefully, Kimble deposited an egg

in James's hand. She gave a small 'wuff' then waddled away back to the hay.

Mandy laughed at the expression on her friend's face. 'There was a bit in one of the books about a Golden Retriever who used to find and collect duck eggs every day for her owner. Remember? I just thought . . .'

'Mandy! That was brilliant!' said James. 'Look, here she comes with another egg. How many have you hidden?'

'Six!' chuckled Mandy. 'They'll probably still smell new laid to her,' she continued, taking the second egg from Kimble and praising her. 'At least, *five* of them might. Libby Masters brought them round this morning.'

Libby's family kept free-range hens; the Hopes were among their regular customers.

'I don't suppose Kimble minds if they're new-laid, free-range or shop-bought eggs,' said James. 'She just seems happy enough to be fetching them.'

But that was where James appeared to be wrong. Kimble only brought five eggs and when Mandy went to look, the sixth egg was on the grass and not in the hay where she'd put it. 'Kimble found it but she wasn't interested in it!' she called to James.

'Well, she's quite happy again now,' said James, pointing to Kimble. The dog had gone inside and was having a long drink from her water bowl.

'She still isn't very interested in food,' said Mandy. 'And she's not over-keen on drinking milk, even with glucose in to sweeten it.'

'That dog who collected eggs!' said James. 'Didn't she like to eat scrambled egg? I wonder . . . ?'He looked thoughtfully at Kimble.

'Good idea, James. I'll pop through and check with Dad or Simon if it's OK to give her some.'

Mandy was almost deafened when she went through to the waiting room. Mrs Anderson had brought Yindee in and the Siamese didn't like being confined in her carrying box.

'Mandy! Am I glad to see you!' Jean Knox had to raise her voice to be heard over the angry yowls. 'Simon's helping your father with a dog who isn't too keen on having his wound dressed and that noise is driving us all crazy. Mrs Anderson says Yindee will settle all right if we put her in one of our big cages!'

'OK! I'll take her through to the residential unit,' Mandy grinned and grabbed a white coat.

'I'm so sorry about this, Mandy!' said Mrs Anderson, handing Mandy the carrying box. 'Yindee doesn't like being confined in a small space.' She looked really embarrassed as Yindee continued to yowl and a couple of dogs started to yap loudly.

'Don't worry. I'll soon have her in a nice big cage,' said Mandy.

After washing her hands at the little sink in the unit, Mandy carefully opened the carrying box and lifted Yindee out. 'You really are beautiful, even though you're so noisy,' Mandy said. Yindee, her bright blue eyes almost crossed and her brown ears pointing straight up, gave one more yowl and swished her long, dark brown tail from side to side.

When Mandy put Yindee in the cage, along with a catnip toy from the carrying-box, the Siamese gave a tiny 'yow-yow' of approval and began playing with it.

Mandy went back to the waiting area. The door to the treatment room opened just then and a sad-looking basset hound, straining at his lead, almost dragged his owner out. Mandy quickly excused herself from Mrs Anderson and popped into the treatment room to ask her dad about giving Kimble some scrambled egg.

Mr Hope said it would be all right and added that he wouldn't mind having some for his own lunch. So Mandy hurried back to James and the two of them set to work, beating eggs and slicing bread for toast.

'We won't make ours until Mum and Dad come

through,' said Mandy. 'But we could make a small portion now, just for Kimble.'

James nodded. 'If she eats it, she could have some more when we have ours,' he said.

To Mandy's and James's delight, Kimble cleaned her plate. Then she climbed into her box, plumped herself down and fell asleep.

'Whew!' sighed Mandy. 'This morning's seemed like hard work! All that thinking and working things out!' She glanced at James and grinned. 'But if you agree with what else I've been thinking, we've got a lot more thinking to do!'

'Get on with it then!' said James. 'You're not making sense.'

'OK. It's like this. You agree that Kimble must have come from a loving home and that her owner obviously cared a lot for her?'

'Definitely!' James nodded hard. 'You can tell that by the way she acts. She enjoys being petted and spoken to. I'm sure if a dog wasn't used to that it would take a while for it to respond. I still can't believe that her owner has abandoned her!'

'I think it *was* her owner who abandoned her,' said Mandy. 'And I don't think it's anything to do with her having pups. But we'll know that when they're born.'

'How?' asked James.

'If they're pedigree Golden Retrievers we'll know for sure,' Mandy stated. 'Because that would mean the pups' father is a Golden Retriever, too. He'd have been chosen specially by Kimble's owner.'

'Who'd be looking forward to the puppies arriving,' said James.

'Exactly!' Mandy nodded. 'So *I* think there must be a special reason for Kimble being abandoned, and the only way we'll find out what it is, is by . . .'

'Finding the owner!' James finished for her. 'But *how*, Mandy? How can we do that? The only thing we *think* we know about her is that she keeps hens or ducks and lets Kimble collect their eggs! And that's hardly likely to help us!'

'I said we'd got a lot more thinking to—' Mandy broke off abruptly; her eyes growing large as she stared towards Kimble's whelping box.

James spun round. 'Oh, cripes!' he whispered.

Kimble was scrabbling at the newspaper in her box, tearing it up and pawing it into a small mound. As James and Mandy watched, she started panting heavily.

'Kimble?' said Mandy in a low voice. Kimble paused in her scrabbling and glanced up.

'She's got a sort of lost look in her eyes,' said James.

Kimble went back to ripping the paper. Her paws

were moving faster this time and suddenly she gave a couple of anxious whines.

'I'm going for Mum or Dad,' said Mandy.

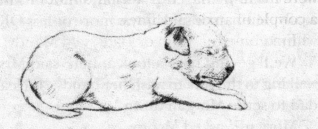

Seven

Mandy dashed out of the kitchen and flew through the door into the surgery like a whirlwind. 'Jean! Is Mum back? Where's Dad?'

'They're in the residential unit,' said Jean. The door was swinging shut almost before she'd finished answering.

'Mum! Dad! I think Kimble's getting ready to have her pups. She's panting really hard and ripping up the newspaper. She looks frantic!'

'She's not the only one,' Emily Hope said kindly. 'Steady down, love. There's usually quite a long gap between the dog making a bed for the pups and actually having them.'

Mrs Hope's matter-of-fact words calmed Mandy

down. She managed a wobbly smile. 'I know that really, Mum,' she said. 'I was more or less OK till she whined.'

'We'll go and have a look at her,' said Mrs Hope, walking to the sink to wash her hands. 'I'll leave your dad to settle Morgan down.'

'Morgan?' asked Mandy.

Adam Hope pointed to a cage. 'A monster of a mouse with an in-growing claw,' he said. 'Yindee must have caught his scent. She started hissing and poor Morgan turned into a mass of quivering jelly. He'll be all right. He's hiding in his sleeping quarters.'

'I'll come and talk to him later,' said Mandy. 'Give him some TLC.' Mandy's parents often said that her TLC – tender loving care – was as good as a tonic.

Adam Hope nodded and smiled. 'That's right, Mandy. Don't keep all your famous TLC for Kimble.'

'I think it will be an hour or two at least before anything happens,' Mrs Hope told Mandy and James after she'd had a quick look at Kimble. 'She'll be feeling rather worried and anxious right now. Becoming a mum is a new experience for her.'

'What can we do to help her, Mrs Hope?' asked James.

'Just let her get on with ripping the newspaper

and don't worry about her panting,' Mrs Hope smiled. 'It's nature's way, James.'

'It's the look in her eyes that gets to us, Mum,' said Mandy.

'Well, don't let it. What she needs at this stage is gentle sympathy. If you two want to stay with her,' Mrs Hope smiled again to soften her words, 'she mustn't be encouraged to feel sorry for herself. Understood?'

Mandy and James nodded. 'That's OK then,' Mrs Hope continued. 'And, James, if you want to stay and see the pups being born you'd better check with your parents. It could be a long job.'

'Do you mean it, Mrs Hope? Can I really stay?' James's face was flushed with pleasure.

'As long as you and Mandy being here doesn't upset Kimble then, yes, you can,' she replied. 'We'll have lunch now, I think, then I'll probably have time to see to Morgan before Kimble's ready to give birth.'

'James and I will make lunch,' said Mandy. 'It's all ready to cook. Dad said he wanted scrambled eggs.'

'Fine. Call us when it's ready. I'll go and see if I can juggle this afternoon's workload round a bit and try and make sure either your dad or I can be on hand. Oh, and if Kimble wants a drink that's all right, Mandy, but I think water or *cold* milk would be better. Sometimes warm milk can make a dog feel sleepy and that could deaden her labour pains. Then she might not recognise when it's time for her to bear down to push the puppies out,' she explained.

'If Kimble couldn't push would you have to deliver the pups by operating on her, Mum?' asked Mandy.

'Possibly, love,' replied Mrs Hope. 'Or, sometimes special injections can help. But don't worry about something that probably won't happen. Most dogs manage perfectly well on their own.'

'Come on, Mandy. Let's get on with lunch,' said James as Mrs Hope left the room. 'It will take our minds off Kimble for a while,' he added.

Mandy smiled. It was really good that James was here with her.

'OK,' said Mandy, when they'd eaten lunch and tidied up. 'We might as well make use of the waiting time, James. Let's make a list of ideas for finding Kimble's owner.'

Mrs Hope had checked Kimble again and told them to call her if there was any change, adding that she'd come back in half-an-hour anyway.

James glanced at the Golden Retriever. 'I know we're not meant to feel sorry for her,' he said. 'But it's hard not to, Mandy. She looks so . . . so . . . far away from us.'

'I know,' Mandy agreed quietly. 'I expect a dog

having her first litter always looks like that. It's probably worse for Kimble because she's in a strange place. That's why we've got to work at this list!'

'Right!' said James, picking up a pen. 'Your parents have contacted all the official authorities so we've got to think of people who come into contact with dogs in other ways. Like the grooming parlour in Walton!' he said, writing it down. 'Jane and Andrew, the owners, don't only groom dogs, they sell pet food. We get Blackie's food from them. They deliver it. They probably cover quite a wide area.'

'James, you're brilliant!' said Mandy. 'They'll know lots of dogs!'

'So they just *might* know Kimble!' said James. 'We could go and see them tomorrow.'

Mandy nodded. 'And there's the travelling library. Everyone chats to Mrs Chambers about their dogs and takes them on the van to see her. And she brings her dog to Animal Ark so we'll have her home number on record.'

'Postmen!' said James. 'They know everybody's dogs. We'll ask our postman to put a notice up in the sorting room and see if he'll get other sorting offices to put one up too! Something like "Do you know the owner of this dog?" with a description of Kimble underneath.'

'And a photograph,' said Mandy. 'We can get a

film for Dad's camera when we go into Walton tomorrow.'

'Now we're beginning to get somewhere!' said James.

'I think Kimble is, too!' Mandy said softly. 'She's squatting, James. She looks as if she's straining a bit. I'll go and fetch Mum.'

Mandy forced herself to walk unhurriedly out of the kitchen and managed to keep calm when she went into the treatment room to fetch Mrs Hope; Jean had warned her that her mother was attending to Morgan. Mandy didn't want to startle either of them.

'All right, Mandy. I've just finished seeing to Morgan. He'll feel a lot better now his claw isn't digging into his pad. You take through some of the small towels, packets of rubber gloves and refuse sacks for soiled bedding. And white coats for you and James,' she added. 'Scrub your hands thoroughly. I'll put Morgan back in his cage and be straight with you.'

James looked really glad to see Mandy. 'Nothing's happening,' he said, as he shrugged on his white coat. 'I was just worried it might.'

'I was only gone a couple of minutes,' Mandy smiled.

'Yes, well, it seemed like ages,' said James, shoving

his glasses further on to the bridge of his nose. 'Kimble's looking at us, Mandy. Do you think she wants stroking or should we leave her alone?'

'We'll ask Mum when she comes,' said Mandy. 'She'll be here soon.'

'She isn't straining for real yet, but I think she soon will be,' said Mrs Hope when she checked Kimble. 'I think maybe she would like you close by. Some dogs like being left alone to get on with things, others like someone within reach. Just kneel or sit by the box and see what she does.'

Kimble stretched her head out and snuffled first at Mandy's shoulder then at James's. Then she moved back, circled the box two or three times and lay down.

'She might feel comfier lying down for the birth,' Mrs Hope said quietly.

'She's stuck one paw over the edge of the box,' whispered James. 'Do you think she wants me to hold it, Mrs Hope?'

'Could be,' Emily Hope nodded. 'You can take it in turns, a few minutes at a time. And I think we should get prepared now.

'Warm water, rags, the small towels and rubber gloves, Mandy, and a cardboard box and heating pad in case we need to separate the pups from Kimble for any reason. Anything else we might need is on my treatment tray on the table.'

Kimble made a small whimper of protest when, after ten minutes or so, James let go of her paw so Mandy could hold it. 'All right, Kimble,' Mandy whispered. 'I'm here for you now.'

A short while later, Kimble's paw jerked, then tensed in Mandy's hand. She turned her head to look up at her mum.

'Mmm, number one pup about to arrive, I think,' Mrs Hope murmured, her eyes on the dog. 'First the water bag,' she continued. It looked like a grey balloon and when it appeared, it burst, releasing a gush of greenish-black fluid. 'Now, hopefully, the puppy,' said Mrs Hope.

The puppy was born wrapped in what looked like a thin covering of dark-coloured polythene. Mrs Hope told them it was called a membrane or sac. James silently pointed to the cord they could see on the tiny creature's tummy. 'The puppy's food came through that when he was inside the mother, didn't it?' he asked quietly.

Mrs Hope nodded. 'The other end is still attached to the afterbirth,' she said. Then she shook her head. 'Kimble doesn't understand what she should be doing. I'll have to show her.'

'What is she supposed to be doing?' asked Mandy.

Mrs Hope glanced very briefly at Mandy and

James, her eyes soft as she noticed their earnest but worried expressions. 'She should be licking the membrane away,' she said. 'Feeling Kimble's tongue would rouse the pup and encourage it to take its first breath. So, the important thing,' she continued, working as she spoke, 'is to tear the membrane over the puppy's nose – pass me a paper towel from my tray, James – then to open its mouth and clear the mucus away with the paper towel and clear its nose as well. Next . . .'

Mandy and James hardly breathed as Mrs Hope held the tiny puppy upside down. 'It allows any fluid to drain,' she explained; then she smiled as the puppy spluttered.

'I'll lay him next to Kimble now and see if she'll take over. There, Kimble, what do you think? Your first-born is a tiny boy pup. Let go of her paw now, Mandy,' said Mrs Hope without changing the steady and comforting tone of voice.

'What should she do now, Mum?' Mandy used the same soft tone. 'Bite off the cord?'

'Mmm, then lick the puppy. But I don't think she's going to do it. I'll have to rub the pup quite hard with a towel. Don't worry if he screams, I want him to. Once Kimble hears him protesting she might take some interest.'

The little pup squealed alarmingly; Kimble got to her feet and James and Mandy looked at each other in delight. It was working!

But it wasn't! Kimble lay down again with her back to them. She just didn't want to know!

'All right, not to worry. The afterbirth came away when Kimble stood up,' said Mrs Hope. 'So *I'll* tie the cord then snip it,' Mrs Hope reached for surgical thread and a pair of surgical scissors from her tray. She tied the cord, then deftly snipped it, leaving about two and a half centimetres attached to the pup.

'We'll pop him in the cardboard box with the heating pad and a layer of towels,' she said.

'What about feeding, Mum?' Mandy asked

anxiously. 'Isn't it important for him to have some milk as soon as possible?'

'It is, but we mustn't force the puppy on her. Not just yet,' said Mrs Hope. 'When the second pup arrives, Kimble might react differently. She might deal with everything herself. Then we can put both pups to suckle at the same time.'

The second puppy was born twenty minutes later. Kimble put her nose close but again she didn't attempt to tear the sac.

'Do you want to do it, Mandy?'

Mandy took a deep breath and nodded. She could hardly believe her mother was trusting her to do such an important job.

'OK. Make sure Kimble can see what you're doing . . . use your thumbnail to break the membrane over the pup's nose . . . that's it. Open its mouth and . . .' Emily Hope passed her daughter a paper towel. '. . . clear the mucus away. And from the nostrils, that's right.'

'Now do I hold the pup head down?' asked Mandy and her mother nodded. This tiny creature didn't splutter, though. It appeared to be lifeless.

'Right. I'll take over.' Mrs Hope took the pup and gently but firmly tapped its rear end. Nothing happened and Mandy heard James swallowing hard.

'This looks cruel,' Mrs Hope warned them. 'But

it sometimes works . . .' And, holding the pup by its back legs, she swung it from side to side.

Mandy bit hard on her lip and James knelt upright, his body rigid, his glasses slipping down his nose. But just then the pup made a noise like a strangled sneeze. They both felt like cheering aloud!

Mrs Hope smiled her relief and Kimble got to her feet and nosed urgently at Mrs Hope's hand. 'She wants it!' Mandy gasped in delight as the Golden Retriever licked the pup from head to tail. 'This time she really does want it. Is it a girl or a boy, Mum?'

'A girl,' said Mrs Hope.

Suddenly the puppy squealed and squealed; James and Mandy looked into the box then, in alarm, at Emily Hope. She laughed at the expression on their faces. 'It's all right, Kimble's not eating the pup. She's bitten the cord off, it often makes a pup yell.'

James took his glasses off and rubbed them on his white coat. 'Whew!' he grinned. 'This is a real nail-biting experience.'

'The pup needs rubbing with a towel,' said Mrs Hope. 'Do you think you're up to it, James?'

James's glasses were back in place in a flash. He took the towel from Mrs Hope, knelt over the whelping box and whispered, 'Don't worry, Kimble. I'm just going to finish drying your pup. I'll put her back in a minute, I promise.'

Kimble watched James with huge anxious eyes and Mrs Hope smiled in satisfaction. 'Hold on a second before you put her back, James.' She reached into the cardboard box for the firstborn pup. 'Her maternal instinct seems quite strong now. We'll put both puppies to suckle together. Ready, James? Here we go.'

Kimble nosed half-heartedly at the boy pup then turned all her attention to the second one. 'She's not too keen on the poor lad, but at least she's letting him feed,' said Mrs Hope. 'Pour some milk, Mandy. We'll leave them for a few minutes then see if Kimble will have a drink herself. Then we'll change the newspapers.'

Kimble lapped eagerly at the cold milk. 'It's the first time she's really seemed to enjoy it,' James commented.

'Are we leaving the puppies in with her while the rest are being born, Mum?'

'Maybe. We'll wait and see. If Kimble gets too restless or there are any problems we'll move them. She's settling herself down, so I think it will be a while before any more arrive. And unless she shows signs of needing us, we'll let her get on with it.'

Mrs Hope popped through to the surgery to check everything was running smoothly. It was time for afternoon surgery; Animal Ark was busy but her husband and Simon were coping.

James and Mandy made themselves milk shakes and sandwiches and sat at the table to discuss their plans for the following day. They decided they'd go to the sorting office and ask about putting a notice up. It would be easier than trying to catch their own postman. After that they'd cycle into Walton, buy a film for the camera, then call in at the grooming parlour.

'We can ask the owners if they know anyone with a Golden Retriever who might be the father,' Mandy suggested. 'I think the pups could be pedigrees.'

'It's hard to tell when they're such tiny scraps and their eyes are closed and their ears are so close to their heads,' said James.

'Mmm,' Mandy nodded but she was more convinced than ever that Kimble's owner had planned for the pups.

She got up to take their used dishes to the sink, glancing into the whelping box as she went past. 'James,' she whispered urgently. 'Kimble's had another pup. She knows what to do now . . . she's tearing the sac herself . . . she's licking the pup all over . . .'

'It's very still,' James said dubiously. 'Do you think it needs shaking like the other one did?'

Mandy heard the door open and turned in relief. 'Mum! There's a third puppy and it isn't moving.'

Emily Hope hurried to the box and lifted the pup. She stared at it for a long second then lifted her eyes to Mandy and James. Mandy's face clouded over. She knew immediately what her mother was going to say.

Eight

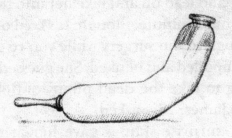

Eight

'This little mite is dead, I'm afraid,' Emily Hope said. She spoke briskly but her green eyes were soft and sympathetic.

'It's a shame it had to happen just as Kimble had learned how to do everything all by herself,' said Mandy in a choky voice.

Her mother nodded and turned her attention to Kimble. 'She's all right,' she said a few minutes later.

'And she's getting out of her box, Mum! Is that because she doesn't want to know the other pups now?'

'She might feel the need to exercise,' said Mrs Hope. 'Some dogs like a little walk round in between pups arriving. She's going to the door, Mandy. Put her collar and lead on and take her into the garden. Only stay out a minute, though. It's cold outside. I'll pop through to the surgery while you're gone.'

Mandy nodded and blinked. She guessed her mum was going to take the dead puppy out of the way. 'Coming, James?' she asked.

To her surprise, James gave her arm a quick squeeze as she opened the door. 'There's still the first two, Mandy,' he said. 'And however many more she has. They'll be all right, just you wait and see.'

'You're right, James. I'll think positively!' said Mandy. And, as they let Kimble walk slowly round the garden, she thought what a good friend James was.

When they went back inside, Kimble wandered over to her water bowl; Mandy and James waited anxiously to see if she'd go to her whelping box when she'd had a drink.

'It's OK, she's going,' said Mandy. They watched Kimble climb in and settle herself down close to the two pups. She licked the girl pup and ignored the boy.

'She doesn't seem to like him at all,' Mandy said sadly. 'Poor little . . .' She glanced at James. 'They ought to have names,' she added.

'How about Jake?' said James, his eyes on the boy pup.

'That was quick!' said Mandy.

James nodded. 'I was thinking about it when we took Kimble outside,' he said. 'Do you like it?'

'Yes, it sounds just right,' said Mandy. 'What do you think of Pippa for his sister?'

'That sounds just right, too,' James replied with a grin.

'There's a strong possibility we'll have to help rear Jake,' said Mrs Hope after she'd returned and put him to suckle. 'Good girl, Kimble, let him have a feed. That's right . . . good dog.'

An hour went by before Kimble showed signs of having another puppy. She started getting restless; standing up, then circling round. 'Let's move Pippa and Jake into the other box, Mandy,' said her mum. 'I know you'd both love to cuddle them but it's best to handle them as little as possible.'

Mandy and James nodded, then quickly but carefully each picked up a pup and laid the tiny bundles side by side in the heated box.

Kimble didn't have any trouble in delivering the next pup but she didn't attempt to tear the sac; she didn't even look at it.

'This one's a boy,' said Mrs Hope, working quickly. 'He's small and weak. I think we'll have a fight on our hands to save him.'

'Felix?' Mandy asked James. 'Shall we call him Felix?'

'OK,' said James. Then he burst out, 'Kimble looks so sad and confused, I hope there aren't too many more pups.'

Mrs Hope was examining Kimble. She glanced up at James, 'Don't worry too much about her, James,' she said. 'Dogs do sometimes react like this when it's their first litter. She'll probably feel a bit happier about things in a day or two. And I can't feel any more pups. I think Felix was the last one.'

A little while later Kimble let Mrs Hope help Felix to feed from her, but showed no interest in him at all.

Mandy sighed. 'Would Kimble be acting differently towards her babies if she was with her owner, Mum?'

Emily Hope nodded. 'Possibly. I'm going to check her over again and change the bedding, then we'll leave her in peace and quiet. She might come round to accepting them whole-heartedly in an hour or so. Meanwhile, Mandy, I think your dad would appreciate a hand in tidying and cleaning up after surgery.'

'I'd better be going,' said James. 'Blackie's seen nothing of me today. He'll be sulking.'

'So will my rabbits,' said Mandy. 'I'll go and see to

them first, Mum, before I go and do my jobs in the surgery.'

Playing with her rabbits, feeding them and settling them down for the night soothed Mandy a little bit. And scrubbing and disinfecting the treatment tables and work tops, mopping the floors and tidying the waiting area helped too.

After a while, Adam Hope joined Mandy in the residential unit. 'Better now?' he asked, ruffling her hair.

Mandy nodded. 'A little bit. I know I shouldn't get so upset when things go wrong. Kimble's got two healthy puppies and the little one *might* make it. I just wish she would show more interest in them. I'm sure she would if she was in her own home. But James and I are going to try and do something about that!' she added determinedly.

'That's my girl,' laughed Adam Hope. 'I'm sure if anyone can do anything, you and James can. Now, Mum wants us to take feeding bottles and some feeding formula with us.' Mandy knew that the formula was especially for hand-rearing. It was as near as possible to the mother's milk, containing everything a puppy needed.

'The tiniest pup is too weak to suckle from Kimble so he's going to need extra feeding and a lot of attention,' Mr Hope continued. 'You can be on duty

till midnight, then Mum or I will take over. OK?'
'OK!' Mandy agreed.

It was hard work trying to coax the tiny puppy to feed
from the banana-shaped feeding-bottle. Mr Hope
had enlarged the holes in the teat so Felix wouldn't
have to suck too hard. But he only took a tiny
quantity before falling asleep.

'If that's all he'll take at a time, we'll have to feed
him hourly,' said Mr Hope. He stroked his beard
and looked at Mandy, his eyes serious.

'I know, Dad,' Mandy sighed sadly. 'We'll be lucky
if he survives. I'm not giving up on him yet, though!'

Mandy tried flicking Felix's back paws gently to

wake him but it didn't work; so she rubbed all round his abdomen with a warm wet piece of cotton wool to help him digest the milk formula and get rid of any waste.

'Shall I put him in with Kimble and the other two, Dad?' she asked.

'Yes. Although she isn't taking any notice of him, she does let him lie close,' said Mrs Hope. 'Snuggling up to her and his brother and sister will give him comfort and help to keep him warm.'

Kimble raised her head to gaze at Mandy when she placed Felix in between the other two. Mandy felt her heart lurch. Kimble looked more forlorn than she ever had before. 'Is she just tired out, Dad?' she whispered, stroking the dog's big golden head.

'There's more to it than that,' Mr Hope replied. 'I think she's missing her home and her owner more than ever. She's OK physically at the moment, but the birth will have dehydrated her and I'd feel a lot happier if she'd drink more. You could try her with some lukewarm milk, Mandy. I'm going to help your mum with some paperwork now. Call us if you need us.'

By midnight, Mandy could hardly keep her eyes open. She'd managed to persuade Kimble to drink a little and she'd fed Felix another three times. He hadn't drunk much, but at least he'd had some.

Kimble had suckled the other two pups. She'd licked and cleaned Pippa each time but ignored the boy pup. So Mandy had rubbed Jake with warm wet cotton wool and he seemed to be OK.

Emily Hope had said goodnight some time earlier. 'Dad's doing first shift, I'll come down at three o'clock,' she'd told Mandy, after hearing the progress report and checking Kimble and the pups.

When Adam Hope arrived to take over from Mandy, she had just made some cocoa. 'I'll take mine up with me,' she said, walking over to have one last look at Kimble and the puppies.

Suddenly, Kimble jumped to her feet. She got out of the box and stood looking up at Mandy. Then she whined!

'What's wrong, sweetheart?' asked Mandy, bending low to stroke the dog.

Kimble raised her head and sniffed; then she tried to reach Mandy's mug. 'Do you want some cocoa?' said Mandy. 'Is that it?'

Adam Hope reached quickly for Kimble's bowl and poured some milk in. Mandy emptied half her mug of cocoa into it then smiled at her dad as Kimble lapped up the whole lot. Feeling a lot happier about Kimble, Mandy made some more cocoa and went up to bed.

* * *

'But your parents do think Jake and Pippa will be OK?' James said. He and Mandy were on their way to the sorting office and Mandy had given him a full report on Kimble and her family.

Felix was still alive but it was a real effort to get him to feed and Mandy knew there wasn't much hope for him.

Mandy nodded. 'Even though Kimble won't have much to do with Jake, she lets him feed. One of us has to clean him and rub him to help him digest the milk, though. She's not over-loving towards Pippa either, but she *is* looking after her. We've just *got* to find her owner, James. I'm sure she'd be a marvellous mum if she wasn't pining so much!'

The man Mandy and James were told to speak to at the sorting office seemed an unfriendly sort of person; Mandy's heart sank when he asked them brusquely what they wanted. She gave him her best smile and explained the situation as briefly as possible.

'Anyone who'd do a thing like that isn't worth being found!' he snapped. 'Surely, if the poor dog had been stolen, the owner could have traced her by now.' He gazed thoughtfully at Mandy, then, to her astonishment, said, 'I'd give her the sort of home she deserves. My old dog was sixteen when she died. I'd had her from a pup. You don't get over losing a good friend and companion that quickly. But it was almost a year ago now.'

'Yes, but . . .' Mandy bit her lip and glanced at James for help. He took over briskly and efficiently.

'Kimble's pining badly,' he said. 'For her sake, and the puppies' sake, it's worth trying to find the owner. We're sure Kimble came from a very caring and loving home and we need to find out what happened to make the owner abandon her.'

'All right. You win. You can bring some notices. I'll put a couple up here and I'll circulate some to other sorting offices. That is . . .' he held a hand up to stem Mandy's flow of thanks, '. . . as long as you guarantee that if the owner comes forward, he or she will be questioned thoroughly before being allowed to have the dog back.'

'If and when we find the owner, the RSPCA will take over,' Mandy told him.

'Fine. That's fine. I'd like you to make it clear on the notice that's what will happen. Perhaps you'd better ask for anyone who has any information to get in touch with their local RSPCA.'

James nodded. 'We'll do that,' he said.

'Good. And make it known that I'd be willing to give the lass a loving home if nobody claims her. Now off you go and get those notices seen to, I'll expect you back first thing tomorrow. And just make sure you get good photos of the dog. We don't want any cases of mistaken identity.'

'I thought we were going to have a big problem with him at first,' said Mandy as they cycled off. 'But he's quite nice under that gruff manner.'

James smiled. Anyone who cared about dogs was OK as far as he was concerned. 'You do realise we'll have to go and buy the film, come straight home and take the photos, then go back into Walton to get them developed?' he asked.

Mandy glanced questioningly at him.

'Otherwise,' James pointed out, 'we won't have the photos in time to take the notices to the sorting office tomorrow morning. If we don't take them then, he's likely to change his mind.'

'It's no problem, really,' said Mandy. 'Apart from making the journey twice,' she added with a grin. The road to Walton was a hilly one! 'Then,' she continued, 'we can call in at the grooming parlour while we're waiting for the film to be developed.'

When they got back to Animal Ark, Mandy made up some milk formula to feed Felix, while James took some photos of Kimble. Mr Hope's camera was easy to use; it automatically adjusted itself, so James didn't have to worry about getting the pictures in focus.

'He's all skin and bone, Dad!' sighed Mandy as

she cradled Felix in the palm of her hand. 'He won't lick my finger when I run it round his mouth and I've put a tiny drop of milk on his nose but he isn't wrinkling it or anything! He's just lying here helpless and I can't help him!'

'The little fellow's getting weaker,' said Mr Hope as he watched Mandy gently squeezing the corners of the pup's mouth, trying to help him suck at the teat. 'I'll go and fetch a syringe. We might be able to dribble a drop of milk into his mouth with that.'

Mr Hope returned, emptied the milk from the bottle into the small plastic container he'd brought as well, then filled the syringe a little way.

'OK, love, put your hand under his chin to support it. I'll see what I can do.'

Mandy watched hopefully as her dad held the end of the syringe that looked like a miniature plastic straw against one corner of Felix's mouth. 'Is it easier for him to swallow if the milk goes in through the side of his mouth?' Mandy asked.

Mr Hope nodded. 'This tiny tube bit is at a slight angle, pointing towards the back of Felix's throat,' he said. 'So, as long as I don't press the plunger too hard and release too much at once, there's less chance of the milk just trickling straight out again.'

'He swallowed then, Dad. I felt his throat move,' said Mandy.

But when Mr Hope carefully released another drop of milk it trickled back out almost straight away.

'Poor little Felix,' whispered Mandy as she dabbed gently at his mouth with some cotton wool. She gave a deep, sad sigh and looked across at James. 'Take a photo of him, James,' she said huskily. 'When we find Kimble's owner we'll at least be able to show her a picture of the youngest pup.'

Adam Hope nodded and squeezed her shoulder. 'I think the other two will make it through all right,' he said. 'We can't win every time, you know. No matter how hard we try.'

'I know, Dad. It still hurts though! Still, there's all the other animals to think of.' Mandy gave him a wobbly smile. 'What's new in the surgery. Any admissions?'

'Yes. One of Johnny Foster's guinea-pigs. It had a nasty splinter in its cheek. Simon got the splinter out, but we're keeping Brandy in overnight to make sure there's no infection. Morgan the monster mouse is going home later and your mum is taking blood samples from Yindee right now.'

'Did Libby bring any more eggs?' asked Mandy after she'd put Felix into his heated box. 'Kimble's going towards the back door. If she wants to go out it might cheer her up if we hide a couple in the hay for her to retrieve.'

'Yes, they're in the pantry,' said Mr Hope. 'We'll make some scrambled egg for Kimble to eat. She needs some nourishment. She's not had much to drink. Even cocoa wouldn't tempt her this morning.'

So Mandy fetched two eggs and hid them in the hay. Kimble collected them when Mandy asked her to. But she didn't wag her tail either time when she dropped them into Mandy's hand.

James watched with a sad look on his face. Then he said abruptly, 'I can't bear to see her like this. We've got to find her owner. Let's get this film back to the chemist's, Mandy. The sooner we do that and get to the grooming parlour, the better!'

Nine

At the grooming parlour neither Jane nor Andrew, the two owners, recognised the description of Kimble. 'We don't have many Golden Retrievers in for grooming,' said Jane, who was busy clipping a black poodle. 'We deliver pet food to one house where there's one. He's won lots of prizes and he's fathered quite a few litters. But he's getting on a bit now; I shouldn't think he could be the father.'

'We'll ask his owner if she's ever seen a dog like Kimble at any of the shows,' said Andrew. 'I know she still goes to them, even though she doesn't enter her dog any more. If you let us have a photo, we'll show it to her and anyone else we can think of.'

Mandy smiled her thanks and asked Andrew if it

would be OK to stroke the dog he was combing out.

'He's terrific, isn't he!' said James. 'I always think Chows look so dignified.'

'He's called Leo,' Andrew told them. 'It suits him, doesn't it? He does look like a lion.'

'Does he live locally?' asked Mandy. 'I've never seen him around. He doesn't come to Animal Ark.'

'He lives in Sheffield but his owner works in Walton and brings him in once a month,' said Andrew. 'He's quite taken to you, Mandy,' he added, as Leo licked Mandy's hand. 'Would you like to finish combing him out?'

'We need to come back here anyway with some photos,' said James when Mandy hesitated. 'You stay here and groom Leo while I go to the chemist.'

'So,' Mandy said to her parents a couple of hours later, 'Jane and Andrew have got a photo to show around and James has gone home to make the notices for the sorting offices.'

It was almost time for evening surgery. Mr and Mrs Hope were having a quick cup of tea before it started and Mandy was preparing a feed for Felix as she talked.

'I'll phone Mrs Chambers later,' she continued, 'and ask her if anyone who uses the library van has a dog like Kimble and if none of that works . . . Well,

I can't think of anything else at the moment!'

'The pair of you have certainly come up with some good ideas.' Emily Hope walked over to look at Kimble who was lying quietly with her puppies. 'Let's hope one of them produces a result. Kimble is really down in the dumps.'

Adam Hope nodded. 'See if you can persuade her to drink some milk or cocoa after you've fed the pup, Mandy. If she doesn't start taking more fluids soon we'll have to put her on a drip to prevent dehydration.'

'If that happens, would we have to bottle-feed Jake and Pippa, Dad?' Mandy asked.

'We may have to anyway,' Mr Hope replied. 'I've got a feeling the poor lass is on the verge of rejecting them completely.'

When her parents had gone through to take surgery, Mandy sighed and looked sadly down at Kimble. Then she shook her head. *I mustn't let her see I'm worried*, she thought. *It might make her worse.*

Mandy tried hard to keep calm and cheerful but it was hard work; the tiniest pup hadn't taken much milk and Kimble moved out of the box when the other two started suckling from her.

'I expect you're thirsty, Kimble,' Mandy said encouragingly. 'Let's have some cocoa, shall we?'

Kimble was lapping half-heartedly at her cocoa

when there was an urgent hammering on the back door. Mandy hurried to open it and Elise Knight dashed in with Jet in her arms and Maisy walking behind.

'I came the back way because it's quicker,' she gasped. 'Jet's swallowed one of my pearl earrings, Mandy! It was my fault. She knocked it off the sideboard and started playing with it. When she picked it up I tried to get it out of her mouth. But she swallowed it. I'm so scared it will get stuck somewhere inside her.'

'How big's the earring?' asked Mandy taking the black cat from Elise.

'I've brought the other one,' Elise gave it to Mandy.

'OK, I'll take her through to the surgery,' said Mandy. 'Don't worry, Elise, it's not a very big pearl, I expect they'll just have to give Jet something to help her pass it.'

When Mandy returned to the kitchen, she smiled reassuringly at Elise. 'Mum says not to worry, she'll give Jet some castor oil. She says leave her with us for tonight, though and—' Mandy broke off with a gasp as she noticed what Maisy was doing.

The Dalmation was sitting close to the whelping box, staring down intently, her head on one side. 'She's looking at the puppies!'

'Puppies?' Elise asked. 'Whose?'

'Kimble's.' Mandy pointed to the Golden Retriever. Kimble was lying down by her bowl, her big head resting on her front paws as she gazed mournfully into space.

'I was so worried about Jet I didn't even see her,' said Elise. 'What's wrong with her, Mandy? She looks so sad!' Then she added urgently, 'Maisy's got her head right in the puppies' box! Kimble won't like that! She might go for her.'

'I don't *think* she will,' said Mandy. 'She's too sad to bother. But I'll keep an eye on her while you get Maisy.'

'OK!' Elise took a couple of steps forward then paused. 'Maisy's licking the puppies,' she said, glancing across at Mandy.

Mandy nodded. 'Just take it nice and slow,' she replied quietly. She knew Elise was trying to work out the best way of moving the deaf dog without making her jump.

But before Elise had time to move again, one of the pups squeaked.

Kimble was on her feet and at the whelping box in a flash, the instinct to protect her litter suddenly strongly aroused. She barged into Maisy, pushing her away, and climbed into the box.

Elise took hold of Maisy's collar and Mandy froze and held her breath.

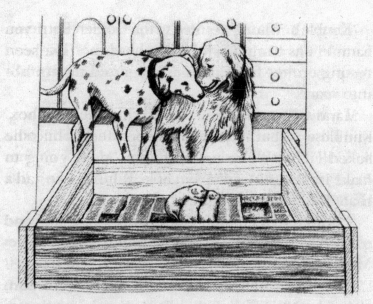

Then she said, 'Kimble's licking them. *All* of them!' Half-laughing and half-crying she watched Kimble's pink tongue working its way over the pups' squirming bodies. Even tiny Felix was squirming a bit. One of them was whimpering with pleasure but Mandy couldn't tell which it was. She didn't dare go too near.

Maisy's tail was wagging and it brushed against Mandy's leg. 'Oh, Maisy!' Mandy knelt down and held the Dalmatian's head in her hands. 'You're a good, good, clever girl. You've made Kimble realise that she does love her puppies after all!'

Elise shook her head in bewilderment. Mandy

grinned, then told her the whole story. 'So if you hadn't had to bring in Jet, Maisy wouldn't have seen the pups and Kimble wouldn't be loving them like she is now!'

Mandy glanced again towards the whelping box. Kimble was letting Jake and Pippa feed while she licked Felix. 'We're not sure that one is going to make it,' she said sadly, 'but at least he'll have had a bit of love from his mother!'

'Oh, Mandy!' Elise gave her a quick firm hug and dashed away a tear.

Adam Hope came in a few minutes later to tell Elise that Jet had been given a dose of castor oil and, all being well, Elise would be able to take her home first thing in the morning.

'Should I go and see her or not?' Elise asked him. 'I don't want to upset her.'

'I should leave her,' advised Mr Hope. 'She's in a cage next to Yindee. They're "talking" away to each other. A right pair they are,' he said. 'A wool-eater and a pearl-eater. Yindee's test results are all OK,' he added to Mandy. 'So I guess the wool-eating is just a habit!'

'Let's hope she doesn't give Jet any ideas then,' chuckled Mandy.

'You look like a cat who's swallowed the cream, Mandy,' he said, noticing Mandy's happy expression.

Mandy nodded and told him what had happened. Maisy gruntled with delight when Mr Hope took her head in his hands to praise her. 'We'll send for you if Kimble loses interest in her pups again,' he told her, his mouth close to one ear so she could feel the vibration of his voice even though she couldn't hear it.

'Maybe she won't have time to lose interest again,' said Elise. 'Maybe Mandy and James's efforts to find her owner will pay off quickly.'

'Oh, I do hope so,' sighed Mandy. 'Once I've phoned the librarian and James and I have taken the notices to the sorting office, we won't be able to do anything but wait!' Mandy was never very good at just waiting for things to happen; she liked to be doing something to *help* them happen.

Elise and Maisy left and Mandy glanced up at her father. 'I was about to feed Felix before all that happened,' she said. 'Should I try now, Dad, or leave him while Kimble's loving him?'

'Being licked by Kimble could just stimulate him enough to give him the incentive to take some milk,' he replied thoughtfully. 'But I doubt he's up to suckling yet.' He crouched down and spoke softly to Kimble as he stroked Felix with one finger. Kimble didn't stop licking the pup but she wagged her tail and didn't try to nudge Mr Hope's finger away.

'I don't think Kimble would mind if you tried feeding him from the syringe while she's licking him,' he said.

So Mandy half-filled the syringe and knelt down by the box. 'Is this OK, girl?' she asked Kimble. 'Can I try and feed your pup? There, I'll put one hand under his front paws so I can hold his head up a bit with my thumb . . . That's right, you lick his tummy. Now I'm going to put this in his mouth. It's got milk in, see?'

Kimble gave a small whine then licked Mandy's hand before returning her attention to licking Felix's tummy.

'It's working, Dad!' Mandy whispered after a while. 'I felt his little throat move when he swallowed then. That's it, Felix. Swallow again . . . and again . . . His tongue's moving now. He's getting the idea, Dad. He's taking quite a bit. And now he's wrinkling his nose. Whoops!'

Mandy chuckled as Felix sneezed. Kimble pushed Mandy's hand away with her paw then sniffed anxiously around the pup's mouth and nose. 'He's all right, Kimble. I haven't hurt him,' Mandy assured her.

Kimble sniffed and licked for a while then she scooped Felix along with one paw and tucked him firmly against her tummy next to Pippa and Jake.

'She's telling me that it's time for Felix to sleep,' said Mandy. 'I'll give him some more in an hour or so. Kimble looks a bit happier now, doesn't she? But she's still got that sort of questioning look in her eyes. As if she's wondering what she's doing here.'

Adam Hope nodded. 'I'm almost sure the pups are pedigree Goldens,' he said. 'So that makes it likely that Kimble was abandoned for a reason other than her being pregnant.'

'We've got to try and find out what that reason was!' said Mandy. 'Oh, I still haven't phoned Mrs Chambers.' She glanced at the clock. 'I'll do that now. She should be home from her library round.'

'Remember, Mandy,' said Mr Hope, '*if* Kimble's owner is traced, it will be the start of another long haul.'

'At least we'd have something else to start *on*!' said Mandy. 'OK, I know,' she added, catching her dad's warning glance. 'It'll be down to the RSPCA. But you never know, they might need a spot of help.'

Ten

Mandy dashed downstairs, brushing her hair as she went. She'd over-slept and she and James had arranged to meet early to take the notices to the sorting office. They were going to walk there and take Blackie with them.

I'll have to feed Felix first, though, she thought, hurtling into the kitchen.

'Morning, Mum. Morning, Dad,' she said, walking towards the whelping box.

'Hang on a minute, Mandy,' Mrs Hope said quietly.

Mandy stopped dead. Her heart sank as she saw the look on her mum's face. 'What's up?' she whispered. 'Something's happened, hasn't it?'

Emily Hope nodded. 'Yes, it's bad news, love,' she

said. 'I'm afraid Felix died about an hour ago.'

'Oh, Mum!' Mandy walked slowly to the table and sat down. 'I know we didn't expect him to make it at first,' she said. 'But then when Kimble started mothering him properly and he started taking some milk . . .' Mandy felt her heart was breaking. Anguished, she turned to look at her mum.

'He took quite a lot from the syringe every time I fed him last night. He even—' Mandy gulped and dashed her hand across her eyes before she continued. 'He licked my fingers, Mum. He seemed to be getting stronger. I thought he was in with a chance. What happened? Why did he die? Would it have made any difference if Kimble had taken to him straight away?'

'I don't think it would have done, Mandy,' said Mr Hope. 'He was just too weak. If he had lived, I doubt he'd have been able to lead the active sort of life a Retriever should. Sometimes, hard though it seems, nature does know best.'

Mandy nodded. She knew her dad wasn't saying that just to try and make her feel better. Her parents were always honest with her. 'It still hurts when it happens, though,' she said. She looked at her mother. 'He wasn't— Did he feel anything, Mum? Was he in pain?'

Emily Hope's green eyes were misty when she

replied, 'He died peacefully, Mandy.' She reached across the table to give Mandy's hand a quick squeeze. 'He was snuggled up to Kimble. I think she sensed what was about to happen. She was licking him very slowly and gently. One second he was breathing and the next second he wasn't.'

'What did Kimble do when it happened?' Mandy asked, her eyes wide. 'Do you think she was upset, Mum?'

'That's the next thing,' Mrs Hope said. 'Kimble is rather distressed. No,' she added quickly, 'don't go to her, Mandy. She's feeling a spot over-protective of the other two pups at the moment.'

'She growls if we go near,' said Mr Hope. 'So we're best just leaving her completely alone.'

'Is that something to worry about?' asked Mandy. 'Or is it good that she's feeling protective?'

'It could be something to worry about,' Adam Hope nodded. 'She wasn't really eating or drinking enough before. Now, she might well refuse to leave her puppies at all. And if she doesn't like us going near her box, she might not eat or drink from a bowl we put in it. A protective mother dog sometimes loses trust even in people she knows well.'

'And she'll see us as strangers more than ever now,' Mandy said sadly.

'But, thanks to Maisy, at least Kimble cares about

the pups now,' said Mr Hope. 'It could be that instinct will tell her to take nourishment so she can keep feeding them. We'll just have to wait and see.'

Mandy sighed. 'It's like taking one step forward then two steps back,' she said.

Her parents smiled and Adam Hope stood up. 'Time for me to take some forward steps,' he said. 'It's my farm round today.'

'Yes, and if I'm going to be on time meeting James, I'd better have my breakfast then get started on my jobs,' said Mandy, reaching for the cereal packet.

James and Blackie were already waiting at the Fox and Goose crossroads. Blackie greeted Mandy with enthusiasm. She cuddled and petted him while she broke the sad news to James about Felix.

'Well, if your parents think it was for the best then I'm sure it was,' said James. 'We've just got to do our very best for Kimble now.'

Mandy gave him a quick smile then gently pushed Blackie down. 'I suppose so, James. But it still makes me feel a little sad.' She admired the notices James had made and they hurried off to the sorting office.

'I just hope the manager hasn't changed his mind about helping us,' said James as they rang the bell on the door of the small single-storey building.

But he hadn't. He even said he'd take a couple of

notices to other sorting offices himself on his way home.

'That's that then,' said James as they walked back up the path and through the gates. 'There's nothing more we can do for now.'

'Then let's go to Lilac Cottage,' suggested Mandy. 'There's an awful lot to tell Gran and Grandad about!'

To Mandy's surprise, the sound of country music greeted them as they arrived at the cottage's back door.

'We're starting square dancing evenings at the village hall,' explained Gran, after she'd greeted James and Mandy and stroked Blackie. 'They hold them in Walton already and a few members of the badminton club have been going. It seemed silly to have to go there when we can hold our own sessions here.'

'That was your gran's decision of course,' smiled Grandad. 'She's organising it all.'

'Which is why I bought the "Teach Yourself Square Dancing" video,' said Gran, waving towards the television. 'I thought I'd better get a bit of practice in before the first session. But that's enough of my news. Sit down and tell us what's been happening at Animal Ark!'

* * *

Twenty minutes later, Gran's phone rang. 'It'll be for you, Dorothy,' said Grandad. 'It nearly always is.'

But when she'd gone to answer the phones Gran called from the hall. 'It's for you, Mandy. It's Jean Knox. Sounds urgent!'

Mandy leaped to her feet and dashed out, followed closely by James and Grandad.

'Jean! Jean! How did you know we'd be here? What's wrong? Is Kimble OK? Has something happened to the pups?' Mandy asked the second she had the receiver in her hand.

Gran, Grandad and James waited anxiously to hear what Jean had phoned about.

'Someone phoned Animal Ark,' Mandy reported quickly, once she'd got off the phone. 'She said the dog is called Kimble and she likes a warm drink of something called "Malto" at eight o'clock every night.'

'Was that it?' said James. 'Nothing else?'

'That was it,' replied Mandy. 'Jean said she didn't have time to mention the puppies. She's sure the call came from a phone box, just like the first one did. That might be to stop us trying to trace the call.'

'It doesn't help, does it?' James sighed as they went back into the kitchen.

'Well, it proves that it was Kimble's owner who left her at the door,' said Grandad. 'Nobody else would know to phone Animal Ark.'

'And we know what to give Kimble to drink,' said Mandy. 'At least, I think we do. I've never heard of Malto.'

'It's a malty powder,' said Gran. 'You pour hot milk on to it, like making cocoa. I used to give it to your dad when he was little, Mandy. He loved it. But I've not seen it for years. I didn't know they still made it.'

'We could see if Mrs McFarlane's got any,' suggested James.

'Right!' said Mandy, leaping to her feet. 'Let's go now, James.'

They said a quick goodbye to her grandparents, James put Blackie on his lead and they hurried off. 'I'll come with you, then take Blackie home,' said James.

Mrs McFarlane ran the Welford post office. Her shop sold all kinds of other things as well – a real general store.

The door squeaked loudly when Mandy dashed into McFarlane's. James was tying Blackie up outside; the door squeaked again as he dashed in after Mandy.

'My, you two seem to be in a hurry,' said Mrs McFarlane.

'Hello, Mrs McFarlane,' panted Mandy. 'We are in a bit of a rush.'

'Well, what can I get you then?' smiled the postmistress.

'Do you sell something called Malto?' asked Mandy.

'It's a malty powder used to make a drink,' James put in.

'I don't stock Malto,' Mrs McFarlane told them. 'But *this* makes up into a malty-tasting drink.' She took a tin off the shelf and passed it across the counter.

'We could try it, Mandy,' said James. 'It might taste the same as Malto.'

Mandy nodded and gave Mrs McFarlane some money. 'Let's hope it does taste the same,' she said.

'Hang on a minute,' Mrs McFarlane called just as Mandy and James were about to leave. 'I've just thought of somewhere where you might get Malto. I can't remember the name of the shop but it's an old-fashioned specialist chemist shop in York. It's down a cobbled side-street just past Mason's, the big furniture shop in the main shopping area.'

'That's great! Thank you, Mrs McFarlane,' said Mandy.

James nodded in agreement. 'If Kimble won't drink this,' he said, 'we could get a train to York tomorrow!'

* * *

A few minutes later, Mandy dashed into the surgery. 'I've got a malty drink for Kimble,' she told Simon breathlessly. 'Do you think it'll be OK to give her some?'

'It's worth a try,' said Simon. 'Your mum looked in at her before she went out on a call. She said Kimble had drunk some water but hadn't touched the milk and glucose. And she still doesn't like anyone getting near her and the pups, Mandy, so I shouldn't talk to her at all. Don't let Blackie anywhere near her, either!'

'It's OK. He's not here,' said Mandy. 'James is taking him home. So, I'll just make the drink, put it as near the box as I can and leave Kimble to it.'

Before long, Mandy was pouring warm milk on to a fawn-coloured powder. It smelt very malty and she glanced at the whelping box to see if there was any reaction from Kimble.

Kimble had her head over the side of the box and Mandy was sure the Golden Retriever's nose was twitching. Moving as casually as she could, Mandy put the bowl on the floor then went outside.

When James arrived, Mandy was peering in the kitchen window. 'I'm watching to see if she'll drink it,' she whispered. 'She's just getting out of the box, James.'

Noses pressed to the window, the two of them watched hopefully as Kimble stretched, then moved towards the bowl. Half-way there, she stopped and turned to look back at the whelping box. Then she moved forward again.

She put her head down to the bowl and sniffed. Her tongue came out and she lapped. But only for a moment. Kimble pushed the bowl away with her nose and padded quickly back to her pups.

Mandy and James sighed so hard, that their breath made misty patches on the window.

'So tomorrow morning we go to York!' said Mandy as they turned away. 'Because even if anyone phones the RSPCA with information about Kimble's owner, Kimble will be with us for a while longer yet.'

'I can't see what good it will do if they do find the owner,' said James. 'If she'd wanted Kimble back she'd have said so when she phoned.'

But Mandy shook her head. 'I *can't* believe she doesn't want Kimble,' she said stubbornly. 'I'm positive there's a mystery here, James. And somehow we're going to solve it.'

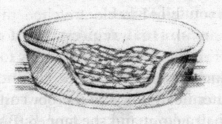

Eleven

'*Apothecary*! Isn't that an old name for a chemist, James?' Mandy pointed to the lettering on the window of a tiny bow-fronted shop on the other side of the narrow cobbled street.

'Yes! That's got to be it,' said James. He let out a huge sigh of relief. They'd spent over an hour searching the side streets of York for the shop. Mrs McFarlane's instructions on how to find it hadn't been too good.

They crossed the road and pushed open the door, smiling when an old-fashioned bell jangled loudly above their heads. The man behind the counter looked like a kindly, ancient wizard with a long grey beard and blue twinkling eyes. He was very strange looking!

'Hello,' said Mandy when she'd found her tongue. 'Please, do you sell Malto?'

'That's an unusual request,' said the man. 'Normally I'd have to order it specially for you. But you're in luck. I got some in for my one and only regular customer. She's a mail-order customer and I send her half a dozen tins at a time. But she phoned to say she wouldn't be needing her order just yet. That was Tuesday. So it will be safe to let you have some.'

'Could we just have three tins, please?' asked Mandy, her voice high with excitement.

'The box is in the back, I'll go and open it up. Have a look round while you're here. I welcome browsers. People tend to think of me when they want something special or unusual. I stock a lot of old remedies, perfumes, herbs, soap, bath cubes, shaving cream, powdered drinks, liquorice roots, herbal candy, cherry gums . . .' He waved in the direction of the tightly packed shelves and went off through a beaded curtain.

Mandy's eyes were shining as she turned to James. 'The order was cancelled on Tuesday!' she whispered. '*One* day after Kimble was left at the door.'

James nodded.

'So are you thinking what I'm thinking?' Mandy demanded.

'Yup! His mail-order customer could well be Kimble's owner. We'll have to lead the conversation round to dogs, Mandy. See what his reaction is. If he's a dog-lover he might be willing to tell us something.'

When the man appeared with the tins of Malto, Mandy couldn't think of a subtle approach. 'Actually, we're buying this for a dog,' she told him as she handed him some money. 'On Monday night someone left her at our door with her lead fastened to a heavy plant pot.'

'We thought she might have been stolen then abandoned,' said James. 'But nobody's reported her missing. She's a lovely dog and she's making herself ill with pining.'

'Then someone phoned, told us the dog's name and said she liked Malto. We were wondering . . .' Mandy gulped before continuing in a rush, '. . . we were wondering if your customer might be the owner!'

The man was silent for a moment. 'Hmm. You could be right,' he said at last. 'She came here once . . . about a year-and-a-half ago if I remember correctly. I think she did mention that she wanted the Malto for her new puppy. I've been sending it to her ever since.'

'That proves it. It is her. It's got to be!' Mandy cried,

turning to James. 'Mum said Kimble is about eighteen months old, didn't she!'

James looked at the man and nodded hard.

'So could you . . . please could you give us her name and address so we can check?' Mandy asked breathlessly.

The man shook his head. 'I'm sorry. I can't possibly give out information like that. It would be a breach of confidence.'

'Just the area where she lives would do, sir,' said James.

'No. No. I'm sorry. It's out of the question.'

'But Kimble might *die* if she keeps pining!' said Mandy. 'Could you phone her and ask—'

Mandy's plea was interrupted by the clanging of the shop bell. 'You'll have to excuse me while I attend to this customer,' the shop owner said as an anxious-looking woman hurried in.

'What are we going to do, James?' whispered Mandy. 'How can we persuade him to help?'

James gave a deep sigh and shook his head.

As the shop owner reached for something from one of the jars behind him, the lady turned to Mandy and James. 'I'm sorry if I pushed in. My young daughter doesn't travel very well and I need something for travel sickness. We've got a long journey ahead of us.'

Before Mandy had time to say anything the door flew open and a boy about James's age said urgently, 'Mum! Mum! Come quick! Barry's got a bone stuck in his throat.'

'Where is he, Jason? Where have you left him? Where's Julie?' the woman asked, hurrying towards the door in a panic.

'I'm here, Mum. What can we do about Barry?' It was a little girl's voice – high-pitched and frightened.

'We'd better go and see if we can help!' The chemist came from behind the counter and, followed closely by James and Mandy, went to the door.

On the pavement at the little girl's feet was a small Yorkshire Terrier. Strange bubbling noises came from his mouth and he was rubbing his face along the ground.

'Poor Barry!' said the little girl. 'He's trying to move the bone.'

'A dog!' said the shop owner, shaking his head. 'I don't think I—'

'A vet! We need a vet!' The lady was crouching down beside the dog. 'I won't be able to remove the bone myself!'

Mandy moved swiftly to the distraught woman and crouched down beside her. 'Don't worry. I think I can help,' she said quietly. She scooped the terrier up into her arms. 'Come on, Barry. Let's get you inside.'

As Mandy walked to the counter, James cleared a space for the dog. Mandy put the terrier down and James moved to hold his body steady.

'It's all right, boy,' Mandy murmured, 'I'm going to open your mouth and look at your throat. There's a good dog. It's OK.'

'Can you see it? Can you see it? Is Barry going to choke?' the woman asked anxiously.

'It's not a very big bone. Barry picked it up out of the gutter,' said Jason.

'Poor Barry!' wailed his little sister. 'Can you get the bone out?'

'Shh!' said Mandy. 'Please don't talk, you'll make Barry struggle.' She looked over to the shop owner. 'Could you let me have a pair of tweezers, please?'

'Are you sure you know what you're doing, young lady?'

'Her parents are vets,' James told him. 'She often helps out in their surgery.'

The man pursed his lips, thought for a while, then disappeared through the bead curtain. When he came back he passed Mandy a pair of tweezers.

A couple of minutes later, with a triumphant smile, Mandy placed the small chop bone on the counter.

James stood the terrier up and the little dog shook his head then looked at Mandy and yapped.

'Yes! It's gone,' she laughed. She turned to the owner and said, 'His gums might be a little bit sore but the bone wasn't digging in too much. It was just lodged across his mouth.'

Jason moved forward to lift the dog then he and his sister cuddled and petted him.

'Thank you so much,' their mother said to Mandy and James. 'I don't know what we'd have done if you hadn't been here!'

'You *are* clever!' said the little girl, looking up at Mandy. 'I guess you must like dogs an awful lot.'

'I like all animals,' Mandy replied with a smile. 'And your Barry is terrific,' she added, stroking the terrier's head.

'He was naughty, though, picking up that horrible bone,' said Julie. 'We never let him have little bones like that! We'd better carry him back to the car in case he finds any more.'

'Yes, and we'd better hurry,' said her mother. 'We'll have overstayed our time at the parking meter.'

She paid for her purchase and, after thanking Mandy and James again, the family hurried away.

The shop owner looked thoughtfully at Mandy and James. 'That was extremely impressive,' he said. 'You've certainly got a way with dogs, young lady.'

'I can't do any more to help poor Kimble, though,' said Mandy. 'Not unless we can trace her owner and find out why she had to abandon her dog,' she added, gazing at him with a look of appeal.

'Hmm. Well. Before you leave, perhaps you wouldn't mind returning the items on my counter to their correct positions!' The man's voice was gruff but his eyes were twinkling. Then he spoke very quickly. 'I believe Kimbleton is a nice village. You should go there sometime.'

'Kimbleton?' said Mandy, an idea beginning to dawn.

'That's right,' said the man, giving a secret smile.

* * *

'I thought Mandy was going to kiss him!' said James. 'I had to grab her and hustle her out of the shop.'

It was six o'clock. Mandy, her parents and James were sitting at the kitchen table watching Kimble drink her second bowl of Malto.

Mandy laughed as she looked at the dog, then towards the door, then back at the dog again. 'I thought I was hearing things when the man mentioned a place called Kimbleton. Then to find it's only twenty miles away from us, and that Simon has an aunt who lives there. Oh, I do wish he'd hurry up!' Mandy's eyes swivelled to the door again, willing the practice nurse to return from phoning his aunt.

Adam Hope smiled and touched his daughter's arm. When she looked at him he put his finger to his lips then pointed. Kimble was padding slowly towards her.

Mandy hardly dared to breathe; a little earlier when she and James had walked into the kitchen Kimble had growled at them from the whelping box. But now... was Kimble ready to be friends again?

'Oh, Kimble,' Mandy murmured softly as the Golden Retriever came and laid her big head on her knee. 'It's all right, girl, everything's going to be all right. Will you let me stroke you now?'

Mandy slid her hand slowly towards Kimble's nose.

Kimble nuzzled into it and wagged her tail. Then she turned and went over to the whelping box. She climbed in, settled down with a 'gerrumph' and licked her two puppies all over.

'Aunt Hannah does know Kimble's owner!' said Simon, coming into the kitchen. 'She's called Vera Morley and she lives alone in an isolated cottage. Aunt Hannah hasn't seen her for a week or so, but she knew Kimble was having pups so she thought Vera was staying in to be on hand.

'My aunt just can't believe what's happened,' Simon continued. 'She said Vera thinks the world of Kimble. Apparently, she is a real animal lover, which is how she knew about Animal Ark. Aunt Hannah told her I work here.'

'So what do we do now?' asked James.

'We should let the RSPCA know and leave it to them,' Adam Hope replied. He glanced at his wife and raised his eyebrows.

'We should,' Mrs Hope confirmed. 'But maybe this Vera Morley would find it easier to explain things to one of us first.'

'Mum!' Mandy leaped up and threw her arms around Emily Hope's neck.

'It will have to be tomorrow. I'm on call this evening and your dad's got an important meeting.'

'And if I don't go now, I'll be late,' said Adam Hope, standing up.

'I promised Aunt Hannah I'd drove over soon for a visit,' said Simon. He glanced at Adam Hope who smiled. 'So it may as well be now then,' concluded Simon. 'Why don't you and James come with me?'

'Simon! That's fantastic!' cried Mandy. She raced over and gave him a hug.

'Is it OK if I phone home, Mrs Hope?' James asked. But his eyes were on Mandy as he moved quickly towards the phone.

Mandy laughed again. 'It's OK, James; I won't hug you,' she promised.

'From what Simon's aunt said about Vera Morley, it sounds as if something quite drastic happened to make her leave Kimble here,' Emily Hope warned, her voice serious. 'But even if the situation has changed since she left her, the outcome of it all won't be up to us, Mandy. You've got to remember that.'

Mrs Hope looked apologetically at Simon. 'It's not that I don't trust you, Simon. It's just that I know Mandy.' She turned back to Mandy and said, 'So no promising her she can have Kimble back. Is that understood?'

'Yes, Mum,' Mandy answered seriously. 'I'll be sensible, I promise.'

* * *

An hour later, Simon drew his van up outside Vera Morley's cottage. There were no street lights in the lane, but an old-fashioned lantern light hanging outside the porch cast a friendly glow over the large front garden. The cottage was low and long with two storeys and there were lights behind the curtains at the tiny downstairs windows.

'Let me do the talking first, Mandy. OK?' said Simon as they got out of the van. Mandy nodded and they opened the wooden gate and walked up the path.

Simon knocked on the door and before long they heard a chain being put into place. The door opened slightly and a small lady with an anxious look on her face and dark shadows under her brown eyes gazed up at them.

Simon explained quickly that he was Hannah Mitchell's nephew. Vera Morley gasped and her hand went to her mouth.

'The one who works at Animal Ark?' she asked, fumbling to release the door chain. Simon nodded and then introduced Mandy and James.

'You've come about Kimble,' said Vera Morley, reaching out for Mandy's hand and almost pulling her in. 'Is she all right? Please tell me she's all right. Has she had her puppies? Oh, you've no idea how worried I've been. I couldn't think of any other safe place to take her. I thought . . . I thought it would just be for a day or two . . . but . . . Oh, you must think I'm so irresponsible and uncaring.'

'Perhaps we could all go and sit down somewhere where you can tell us about it?' suggested Simon.

Vera nodded and led them into the front room.

'I will tell you about it,' she said, once they were all sitting round the fire. 'But, please, tell me about Kimble first.' She pointed to a dog bed on the floor in an alcove next to the hearth. 'You've no idea what it's felt like just staring at Kimble's empty bed night after night. Wondering if she was missing me, wondering if she'd had her pups. She's such a softie at times. I knew she'd need me. I promised her I'd be with her when she had her pups.'

'We were with Kimble when she had her pups!' James burst out. 'Mandy and her mum and me. Kimble was worried and bewildered. Mandy and I held her paw to comfort her and when she had the puppies she didn't know what to do. We had to show her and help her and—' James broke off suddenly as he noticed the tears rolling down Vera's cheeks.

And when Vera looked across to Kimble's bed and murmured, 'Oh, Kimble. I'm so sorry.' Mandy's heart went out to her.

'Kimble had four puppies,' she said. 'There's Jake and Pippa – they're coming on nicely. The third one

was still-born and the fourth one was tiny and weak.
We called him Felix. I'm afraid he didn't make it,
either.'

'But is Kimble all right?' Vera asked and Mandy
glanced across at Simon.

'We think she's going to be now,' said Simon. 'Mr
and Mrs Hope were worried she'd become
dehydrated; she hasn't been eating or drinking as
much as she should. But Mandy and James got her
some Malto this afternoon, like you suggested, and
she had two lots before we came out.'

'Is she enjoying being a mother or is she still
feeling too confused?' asked Vera.

'She didn't take to the pups very well at first,' said
Mandy. 'But then . . .' Mandy went on to tell Vera
about what happened when Maisy had licked the
puppies. 'And after that, Kimble became a really
loving mum. She was really upset when little Felix
died. She wouldn't let anyone go near her or the
pups after that.'

'Until this evening,' said James. 'After she'd had
some Malto, she went over and put her head on
Mandy's knee.'

Vera mopped her eyes, then said, 'I'll tell you why
I left Kimble. Maybe you'll understand even if you
can't forgive me.'

Then Vera explained everything.

She told them she rented her cottage. There was a clause written into the lease stating that no dogs were allowed. But the owner of the cottage had agreed to waive that clause for Vera.

'Mr Samuels had known me for a long time,' she said. 'He knew I wouldn't let a dog wreck the place or go chasing sheep – the fields behind the cottage belong to a sheep farmer. He got to know Kimble well and he knew my sister, too. She died a year ago. She was blind and her guide dog, a Golden Retriever related to my Kimble, meant everything to her. She left me some money when she died and I donated it to the Guide Dog Association. Then I thought it would be nice to let them have a puppy or two to train.'

'Did that make you think about letting Kimble have puppies?' Mandy asked. 'We guessed the puppies had been planned for.'

Vera Morley nodded, then took a quivering breath before continuing. 'Mr Samuels gave me the go-ahead and even said he's like to adopt one of the puppies. But then . . .'

The rest of the story came out in an anguished rush. A month ago, the landlord had been taken ill and been rushed into hospital. His nephew had taken over the management of the business; Mr Samuels owned quite a few properties that he rented out.

There'd never been anything put in writing about Vera being allowed to keep a dog. The nephew told her she'd have to get rid of Kimble or get out of the cottage.

'I told the nephew that his uncle had given me permission to have Kimble,' said Vera. 'But he told me he was in charge now and *he* wasn't giving permission. I ignored him at first. I thought Mr Samuels would soon be back and it would all blow over. But then the nephew told me his uncle had to have an operation.

'And last Sunday morning he came again and said if Kimble wasn't out of here by the next day, he'd deal with it himself. He said the authorities would be on his side. He said they'd come and take Kimble away and rehouse her!'

'But why didn't you go and see Mr Samuels?' asked James. 'You could have gone on Sunday and he could have explained everything to his nephew!'

'I tried that, James,' Vera said, her voice anguished. 'Mr Samuels was very poorly. They wouldn't let me see him. I couldn't think what to do. I knew the nephew would be round first thing the following morning. I was terrified he'd bring someone with him to take Kimble away!'

James took his glasses off and rubbed them furiously on his sweater while he stared into the fire glowing cosily in the hearth.

Vera sighed and ran her fingers through her hair. 'In the middle of the night I suddenly remembered everything Hannah had told me about Animal Ark. I got up early, put Kimble in the car and drove towards Welford. Then, when it was dark, I came and left Kimble at the door,' she whispered. 'I thought she'd be safe there for a day or two while I found somewhere else to live. When I'd done that I was going to come to Animal Ark and explain everything.'

Vera sighed. 'I've spent the whole week going to estate agents and phoning numbers out of newspapers,' she said. 'It was useless. I couldn't find anywhere that would allow dogs.'

'But why didn't you go to Animal Ark and tell Mandy's parents what was happening?' asked James. 'They might have been able to think of something!'

'Believe it or not, I was going to come this afternoon,' said Vera. 'I was just about to set out when the postman came. He said something about a notice that had been put up in the local sorting office late yesterday afternoon. Said there was a photo of a dog just like Kimble on it, and if anyone knew the dog's owner they were to inform the RSPCA. I don't think he dreamed for a minute that it *was* Kimble.'

She glanced sadly at Simon. 'I gave up all hope of everything then. Even if I could find somewhere else to live now, somewhere where I could have Kimble, the RSPCA wouldn't let me have her back. Not after I've abandoned her.'

Vera stumbled out of her chair. 'I don't know how you found out about me. But I'm grateful to you for coming and for everything you've done for Kimble and her pups. But I'd like you to go now. Give Kimble my love, tell her I miss her and, most of all, tell her I'm sorry I let her down. And please, please, try and find her a good home. And the puppies as well, of course.'

Mandy and James looked at Simon for guidance.

Vera looked at Simon too. 'I really do mean it, Simon. There's no other way!'

Twelve

'Do you think we should have left her?' asked Mandy, as they walked back down the path. 'She was so upset!'

'I know,' said Simon. 'But I think if we'd stayed she'd have got even more upset.'

'I think there might be something we can do, though,' said Mandy.

James nodded. 'I think so too.'

'I'm sure we've all had the same idea,' said Simon, as he unlocked the van door. 'And that's to find out which hospital Mr Samuels is in!'

'We need to try and get in to see him before we go back to school on Monday,' said James. 'We won't have much spare time to do anything then.'

'We should have asked Vera,' said Mandy.

Simon shook his head. 'No, we shouldn't have Mandy. I don't want her to know what we're thinking of doing,' he went on. 'Because it wouldn't do to raise her hopes in any way.'

'But *how* are we going to find out where Mr Samuels is?' said Mandy.

'I suppose we could phone the local hospitals and ask if he's there,' said James. 'There won't be many, will there?'

'We need a bit more information before we start phoning around,' said Simon, switching on the ignition. 'Knowing Mr Samuels' first name would be a help. And my Aunt Hannah is sure to know it! So if you belt up,' he joked, pointing to their seat belts, 'we'll go and ask her.'

'It's almost nine o'clock. Isn't it a bit late to go visiting?' asked James.

'Aunt Hannah will be delighted to see us,' said Simon.

Simon's Aunt Hannah was delighted to see them. She led them into the kitchen and said they were just in time for supper. She bustled around making hot chocolate, asked Mandy to make herself useful by cutting some fruit slab and set Simon and James to work – making and buttering toast.

'Eat first, talk after,' she commanded, when she'd seated them all to her satisfaction. Mandy and James grinned and obeyed willingly when Aunt Hannah added, 'Well, tuck in then. What are you waiting for?'

When they'd finished, Mandy said it was the most delicious supper she could ever remember eating.

James agreed. He'd managed to drink two huge mugs of hot chocolate.

'Good. I'm delighted you enjoyed it! Now, get on with it, Simon,' Aunt Hannah said brusquely. 'Tell me what happened to make Vera Morley give up the dog she loved.'

'I know Kenneth Samuels' nephew,' she snorted, when Simon had told her everything. 'He's a really nasty person. He wants Vera's cottage for himself. Always has done, ever since Vera moved in five years back.'

'I suppose it's too much to hope that you know which hospital Mr Samuels is in?' Simon asked.

'Saw him this afternoon with my own eyes,' his aunt retorted. 'I'm a Friend of Highlands Hospital. Today was my day for visiting. Kenneth is still poorly but not so poorly that I couldn't have a bit of a chat. There's nobody else to visit him. The nephew doesn't bother and he's Kenneth's only relation.'

'Well . . .' Simon began. Then he shook his head. 'No,' he murmured. 'Even you couldn't arrange that!'

'Oh, couldn't I, my lad? I'm already one step ahead of you. Needs to be seen, doesn't he? Needs to be told what's going on?'

She looked over at James and Mandy. 'Right, you two. Lay your hands on some paperback books, can you? And a few flowers, maybe, and a bit of fruit? Yes? Right. Be here at two-thirty tomorrow. You two are going to be temporary Friends of the Hospital. Visiting folks who haven't anyone else to go and see them.'

'Like Mr Samuels?' asked Mandy.

'That's right!' said Aunt Hannah with a chuckle.

Next day, Mandy and James felt rather nervous as they followed a nurse down the hospital ward. They were carrying flowers from Grandad Hope's garden, two jars of bramble jelly from Gran's store-cupboard and some paperback books that James's father had let them have.

Simon had driven them to his aunt's house and she'd told them that she'd cleared their visit with the ward sister. Mr Samuels would be expecting them.

But, thought Mandy as they made their way to Mr

Samuels's bed, *he has no idea why we're really here!*

'Think of Vera Morley and Kimble,' James whispered. He'd guessed what was worrying Mandy. Mandy nodded and shot him a grateful glance.

'Your young visitors are here, Mr Samuels,' the nurse said cheerfully. Then she turned to James and Mandy. 'Ten minutes. No longer. OK?'

'OK,' agreed Mandy, hoping that ten minutes would be long enough. There wouldn't be any time to waste!

Mr Samuels thanked them for their gifts, then regarded them quizzically. 'It isn't often that people your age can find the time to do this sort of thing,' he said.

Mandy bit her lip as she met his gaze. 'I'm sorry,' she said at last. 'We *are* here under false pretences, Mr Samuels.'

'But it's because we're trying to help someone!' James blurted out. Then, blushing furiously, he reached into his pocket, pulled out a photograph and handed it silently to Mr Samuels.

'This is Kimble, isn't it? Vera Morley's dog? I'm very, very fond of both of them. I did wonder . . .' Mr Samuels shook his head. 'No reason why she should have come, of course.'

'If you're wondering about Vera,' Mandy said softly, 'she did try to see you, but they wouldn't let her in. You weren't well enough for visitors on the day she came.'

'That's a shame. I would have enjoyed a visit from her. She could have told me all about Kimble. Has she had the pups yet? And—'

Mr Samuels broke off again and looked at James. 'You said you were trying to help someone, young man? I think you'd better tell me what this visit is really about.'

'It's about your nephew,' James said, coming straight to the point. 'He told Vera Morley that she'd have to get rid of Kimble if she wanted to stay in her cottage.'

'That's ridiculous!' said Mr Samuels. 'Surely she told him that I'd agreed to let her have Kimble there.'

'She did!' said Mandy. 'And he told her *he* was in charge and he wasn't giving her permission to keep Kimble. He said he'd get the authorities to take Kimble away.'

'They haven't done that, have they?' said Mr Samuels, his colour rising alarmingly as he sat bolt upright in the bed.

'Not yet,' said James. 'But they might!' And he and Mandy went on to tell Mr Samuels everything else that had happened.

'We saw Vera last night and she's given up all hope of having Kimble back,' Mandy ended.

Mr Samuels heaved himself to the edge of his bed and called loudly for a nurse.

'Mr Samuels! What on earth's the matter?' the nurse asked. 'I hope you two haven't been upsetting him,' she added, glaring first at James, then at Mandy.

'*You'll* upset me, Nurse, if you don't get me to a phone! I've an urgent call to make. And you'll have to allow my friends here a few minutes extra with me. We've a very important matter to sort out.'

'Are you . . . are you phoning your nephew?' Mandy asked when the nurse bustled away to fetch a wheelchair.

'I'm phoning my solicitor. As well as handling my business affairs, he happens to be an old and valued friend. Don't worry, this whole matter will be dealt with immediately!'

Ten minutes later, Mandy and James were dashing across the hospital car park to where Simon was waiting by his van.

'So it was a successful visit!' Simon guessed when Mandy and James skidded to a halt.

'Yes! Yes, it was! Mr Samuels phoned his solicitor and he's changing Vera's lease,' Mandy panted. 'She can keep a dog there now.'

'And Mr Samuels's nephew will be getting a letter

ordering him to stay away from Vera and her cottage,'
added James, shoving his glasses back into place.

'And . . . and first thing tomorrow Mr Samuels and
his solicitor will be phoning the RSPCA Inspector
who handles cases in the Kimbleton area,' said
Mandy. 'They'll both explain what happened and
Mr Samuels will—'

'Vouch for Vera. That's the word he used,' said
James.

'The RSPCA *will* agree to let Vera have Kimble
back, won't they, Simon?' Mandy asked anxiously.

'I should imagine so,' Simon replied thoughtfully.
'But they're bound to pay her a visit to check
everything out.'

The next three days passed slowly. Vera phoned
every day to check on Kimble and the pups; she was
becoming more and more anxious because she
hadn't heard anything from the RSPCA.

Then, on Thursday, when Mandy and James came
out of school, Mrs Hope was parked outside in the
Animal Ark Land-rover. 'Sling your bikes in the
back,' she said. 'We're going to Kimbleton. I've
checked with your mother, James, and it's all right
for you to come.'

'But *why?*' asked Mandy. 'Why are we going, Mum?
What's happened?'

'Vera Morley's had notification of a visit from the RSPCA Inspector,' Mrs Hope told them. 'She phoned Animal Ark to ask if you two could go to lend support. Now, Mandy, you've got to promise me that you'll accept whatever is said. No protest if the decision goes against Vera. OK?'

'But, Mum . . .' began Mandy. Then she relented. She knew from the seriousness of her mother's expression that she meant exactly what she'd said. 'OK,' she whispered. 'I promise.'

'Me, too,' murmured James. 'But it *will* be all right, won't it, Mrs Hope?'

'I don't know the answer to that, I'm afraid, James. We'll just have to hope it will be.'

There was already a car there when they drew up outside Vera's cottage. Mandy didn't know whether to be glad or not.

'If that's the Inspector's car, at least we won't have to wait long before we know!' muttered James.

When Vera opened the cottage door, Mandy looked anxiously at her, trying to judge how things were going. Vera looked pale and worried and didn't speak. She just pointed silently toward the front room.

Mrs Hope introduced herself, Mandy and James to the stern-faced Inspector.

'I was about to impress upon Miss Morley the possible consequences of abandoning an animal,' he said. 'No matter that, in this case, she'd done her best to make sure the dog was unable to run off. It *could* have run off when the lead was unfastened. That could have caused an accident, even death, not only to the dog but to whoever was trying to help the dog. In other words, leaving a dog, even at the door of a veterinary practice, was a highly irresponsible act.'

'I know that,' Vera whispered. 'I know I should have *taken* Kimble and *asked* for help. But what if the answer had been "no"? What would I have done then?'

The clock ticked away as the Inspector regarded Vera in silence. Then came a loud 'cock-a-doodle-doo' and Vera rose to her feet. 'I'm sorry,' she said, 'the hens need feeding and shutting away for the night. It's well past time.'

'Tell us where everything is and James and I will see to them,' said Mandy. She didn't really know how she could *bear* to leave the room without any decision having been made. But the hens were hungry and their routine had been upset.

Before Vera could reply, the Inspector turned to look at Emily Hope. 'Are the dog and her pups well enough to be moved?' the Inspector asked Mrs Hope.

Moved to where? Mandy wanted to ask the question aloud but she knew she couldn't. She only vaguely heard her mother's confirmation; she was watching Vera stumbling back to her chair.

'Perhaps, Mandy, when you and James have fed the hens, you'd like to go back to Animal Ark in Miss Morley's car,' said the Inspector. 'I'm sure she'd like to fetch Kimble and the puppies and get them settled in their own home as soon as possible.'

To Mandy's horror, Vera Morley said, 'No, Inspector. I won't be going to Animal Ark. Not today,' she added quickly, wiping away the tears. 'Tomorrow morning, can I come tomorrow morning?' she asked Emily Hope. 'The waiting will be awful but I wouldn't dare bring them home in the dark. I'd be scared of having an accident.'

'Come back with us now, Vera,' said Mrs Hope. 'You can stay the night. I'm sure Mandy will be delighted,' she added, throwing a smiling glance at her daughter. 'You can sleep in the spare room.'

As they walked down the hallway to Animal Ark's kitchen, they heard anxious and excited whines and frantic scratching noises at the closed door.

'She's recognised my footsteps!' cried Vera, running forward. 'I'm coming, Kimble. I'm here!'

The whines turned to yelps of joy when Vera opened the door. Kimble didn't jump up; she didn't need to. Vera knelt down and flung her arms around Kimble's neck. In between whining and yelping, Kimble licked Vera's face and neck and ears.

Mandy, James and Mrs Hope stood in the hall, smiling as they watched the reunion.

'Oh, Kimble! Kimble,' Vera murmured. The dog stayed still for a moment, her big golden head resting on Vera's shoulder.

Then Mandy drew a sobbing breath and whispered, 'Mum! Kimble's crying. I didn't know a dog could cry real tears.'

'Oh, dear,' said Emily Hope. 'I think I need a hanky.'

'Me, too,' said James taking off his glasses and blinking hard.

Then Kimble moved. She got hold of Vera's jacket in her mouth and started tugging. 'I think she wants to show Vera her puppies,' said James. 'I don't want to miss this. Will it be OK if we go in, Mrs Hope?' Emily Hope nodded.

Kimble's tail was wagging furiously as she led Vera to the whelping box. Vera knelt down again and, after murmuring something to Kimble, she picked the puppies up. 'They're beautiful, Kimble,' she said as she stroked and examined them. 'Aren't you a clever girl?'

Kimble lay down and put her head on Vera's knee. 'What did you say you'd called the puppies, Mandy?' Vera asked over her shoulder. 'Jake and Pippa?'

'Yes, but we won't mind if you want to re-name them,' Mandy replied.

'Oh, no!' said Vera. 'We couldn't do that, could we, Kimble? Just move your head for a second, girl. I'll put your pups back then I want another look at you. I've missed you so much.'

Vera leaned forward and lay the puppies down. 'There you are, Jake,' she said. 'You snuggle close to Pippa.'

As Vera waited to make sure the puppies were settling, James glanced at Kimble. The dog's eyes were fixed adoringly on Vera.

James took a huge, long breath then turned to Mandy and said, 'I'm going now, Mandy. I think I want to get home and spend some time with Blackie.' He gave a last, lingering look at Kimble, saying a silent but happy goodbye.

Vera didn't sleep in the spare room after all, but on a camp bed in front of the stove in Animal Ark's kitchen. She just couldn't bear to be parted from Kimble. Kimble and the puppies slept on the camp bed, too. Vera apologised about that when Mandy crept into the kitchen early Friday morning.

'I tried to make Kimble keep Jake and Pippa in the box,' she said. 'But every time I moved them, she just picked them up and put them on the bed again.'

'It's OK,' said Mandy, smiling as she looked down at the contented family. Then she looked closer. 'Vera,' she whispered, 'the puppies' eyes are starting to open! I'm sure they are. It must be because they know they're going home.'

Three weeks later, Mandy heard a muffled thump coming from outside the front of the house. She opened the door to find Kimble standing there. But this time, the dog at the door wasn't tied to a plant pot, she was holding a small card in her mouth.

Mandy bent down to cuddle Kimble, then, keeping one arm around the dog's neck, she removed the card and read it. '*Vera Morley and Kenneth Samuels request the pleasure of Mandy Hope's and James Hunter's company at their wedding . . .*'

Mandy stood up with a smile of delight as Vera and Mr Samuels, each carrying a wriggling puppy, came from behind a bush. 'You will accept, won't you, Mandy?' asked Vera, blushing a becoming shade of pink. 'You and James *will* come to our wedding?'

'Of course we will!' said Mandy, moving forward to stroke the puppies.

'And,' Mandy said to James when she phoned him later, 'I know just where we can go to buy Vera and Mr Samuels a wedding present. A little old-fashioned apothecary in York!'